In Body I Trust

In Body I Trust

A Novel
by

Lauren Dow

New Luna Press
DENVER, COLORADO

Cover Design Copyright © 2021 by Lauren Dow
Book design and production by New Luna Press, LLC
Edited by Claire Evans
Book cover photograph by Timmy Miller
This book was professionally typeset on Reedsy.

New Luna Press is a registered Limited Liability Company and is a trade name of New Luna
Press, LLC.

PRINTED IN THE UNITED STATES OF AMERICA
Library of Congress Control Number: 2021901989
Description: Denver, Colorado : New Luna Press, 2021
ISBN 978-1-7365725-0-4 (paperback) | ISBN 978-1-7365725-1-1 (hardcover) |
    ISBN 978-1-7365725-2-8 (ebook)

newlunapress.com
laurendow.com

Content Warning: The following content of this book discusses topics regarding eating disorders, mental illness, self-harm, and suicide.

For the ones who suffer in silence, you are not alone.

Contents

Preface

What *will I leave behind?*
        I used to believe in the false narrative that the world
        should exist without me in it, that there was no future
beyond age twenty-nine when I attempted to take my own life.

I'm not sure when it all started—the impulsivity during a state of
anxiety and over the top emotional highs, the deep depressive spells
that sucked me into bed for days on end, or the disordered eating
thoughts and behaviors which dictated my life for years. However,
recovery is not a linear process with a clear beginning or an obvious
end.

When I originally started writing this book, it was a means of
Cognitive Behavioral Therapy suggested by my therapist. I wrote
in *"I"* statements and worked through a cyclical motion of different
emotional scenarios to dissociate feelings from food. I was trying to
discover what control really meant to me and learn how to navigate
this world of recovery alone. I had to know what it would take to come
out the other side alive.

It was never intended for anyone's eyes but mine.

But as I continued to write, the masks I wore every day were slowly
removed. I was tired of hiding behind a façade. I made the decision
to share my experiences on my blog and social media. I soon realized
there were far too many others who were experiencing the exact same

1

thing, regardless if there was a diagnosis or not. A blog would not be enough. I turned my personal, therapeutic word dump into a book. I shifted the story to a third-person perspective. By removing myself personally from the narrative, I became a viewer of my life instead of the one living it. I turned my eating disorder into a living, breathing person with a face, a story, and a name.

What you'll see throughout this book is what lies behind an average day in the life of someone with disordered thoughts, someone for whom mental illness has become their driving force. You'll be exposed to parts of myself I never thought I'd share because I believed there was no point. But now, I understand that I needed to fall in order to show others that it's absolutely possible to get back up.

This book is a transparent and authentic depiction of who I am and what I've overcome. It's the realization that it was never about body image or my weight. It was something rooted far deeper below this leafless tree I called a body.

The characters you'll meet are not one specific person, but rather conglomerations of the every-friend, the multiple abusers I've been with, the embodiment of loneliness through mental illness, and the truth behind my personal journey of recovery.

As a special note to those who suffer from mental illness and eating disorders, I love you. I unconditionally adore you for exactly who you are. I wrote this for you. I wrote this so you would know you're not alone. Recovery is possible. It's a lonely road but it leads to somewhere beautiful. It's a vista you can experience, too.

Before you continue reading, take a second and breathe. Open your eyes to see the world around you for what it really is. It's not about what happened five minutes ago, it's not about what happened five years ago. It's about what's happening right now and how you plan to move forward.

It's like hiking a trail in the mountains. Eventually there will be a fork in the path where you'll have to make a decision. You can take the clear, definitive trail you've seen time and time again but leads you nowhere new. Or you can take a turn off the beaten path, towards the thin trail covered with overgrown trees and brush, the one without any indication of where it's going. It might seem daunting, but you're never going to know how epic the destination might be until you try.

Don't punish yourself if you're afraid to take the uncharted path just yet. Don't beat yourself up because you need to walk that steady, clear, concrete trail ahead of you for a little bit longer. Someday you'll find the strength and vulnerability to explore the wilderness. And no one else will be able to do that for you except yourself.

I fought tooth and nail through recovery to be able to enjoy the simplistically beautiful things life has to offer. All I want is to bring a sliver of that light into someone else's darkness.

When you're ready, walk that path with your eyes wide open. Put your heart out into the world, live through the wisdom of your higher power, and lead with love. The rest will fall exactly into place.

This book has given me the gift of closure. This book is what I will leave behind.

Chapter 1

I n the morning, she thrived. She had her routine and a sense of optimism. Determination fueled her body, but typically ended around noon when the day finally turned over. Not on days like this. Days like this were a taste of paradise. A vacation from the norm.

Brisk air and a gray haze covered the city, making the world feel like it would be morning all day long. A haze that silenced the voices of her eating disorder. They too were on a vacation from the norm as they lazily napped in the back of her mind. Amelia could finally take a moment to breathe.

The clouds hovering outside her bedroom window reminded her of the northwest. Maybe she'd do better living somewhere like Portland or Seattle, but she associated those places with debilitating depression. A curse she already had to manage daily. But...what if she was wrong? Maybe she could move to one of those sleepy cities and it would silence the voices for good.

Every year since she graduated college, Amelia would sell everything she owned and move somewhere new. She'd drive around the country with the hope of finding a way to start over. She didn't view it as running away, but rather running towards something: a sense of home.

Even her new apartment felt foreign to her. A giant marble placard hung outside the front door of the four-story shared townhome. *Built in 2004.* Not even old enough to drink. It had its quirks which she loved and was perfectly located in the heart of Denver. Still, it wasn't home. More like an extended stay at a fully furnished Airbnb.

The line between normal spontaneity and manic episodes resulting in destructive impulsivity was a thin one; Amelia was never sure on which side of the line her decisions to move fell. At least that's what her therapist, Miranda, told her.

"You seem to revisit the idea of moving a lot," Miranda said in their last therapy session. "You've switched apartments three times in the last year, and now you're considering moving back to Florida with your mom again."

"Right, but it's not like I have anything here for me—"

"Since Dominic left," Miranda interjected.

Amelia hadn't yet figured out who she was without him. She'd met Dominic right as she was dramatically planning her first solo backpacking adventure. Six continents in one year. That was the plan, at least it was the plan before that night they met. After hours of flirting at Scottie's Pub and getting three whiskey gingers deep, she leaned in close so he'd hear her words over the beating music. The words that would change both of their lives forever.

"Are we going to pretend like this isn't happening?" Dominic was taken aback by her boldness. Without overthinking, he leaned in closer, held her face with both hands, and kissed her while the rest of the bar faded away.

Home. Is this what home feels like?

Only this time, instead of running away to find home, home would come with her. He ordered his passport and bought a one way ticket to Paris with Amelia.

It took nine months of traveling for Amelia's depression to find her again. She expressed to Dominic her need for stability, which is how they settled on Denver as their new home. But within a few hours of returning back to the United States, Dom had thrown away almost two years of sobriety with a few bumps of crushed oxycodone through his nose.

After another year and a half of codependency and toxic fighting, Dominic performed his final act of manipulation. He went on a "vacation" to Guatemala and never came back. He left her alone with Luna in an apartment she didn't want, in a city that made her feel like a constant stranger. He abandoned her.

Even thinking about Dominic made her question if their relationship had been a legitimate desire or her mania. Her gut had sent out warning signs and her close friends suggested there were red flags, yet she still fell into an overly romanticized version of backpacking the world with him. Anorexia was just collateral damage.

"Bipolar disorder is a complicated thing." Amelia felt Miranda was hinting putting her back on medication. "It's easy to confuse being spontaneous and being impulsive. It's like having to choose a side, only you don't know which side is telling the truth. So you fall into your eating disorder because at least you know it's one thing about yourself you can control."

"So I'm bound to live in a catch-22 for the rest of my life?"

"What I'm saying is that maybe the reason you've had a difficult time with basic decisions is because you're too overwhelmed by the big ones."

Simple decisions were like mountains she had to climb barefoot in a blizzard. The voices would take over, blasting at full volume, and she followed their orders every time. It was easier that way. Her rational brain was too debilitatingly indecisive for her to argue with.

Amelia rolled over on her side to be the big spoon to Luna's little. She rubbed her face along the back of Luna's freshly washed fur, the feeling a balm for her anxiety.

They snuggled in bed while Luna's tail wagged with excitement until the apprehension of not immediately seizing the day took over, forcing Amelia out of bed. She pushed the forty-pound puppy aside to fix the sheets, removed her glasses and replaced them with contacts to see the world for what it really was. Just another Monday.

Amelia continued with her morning ritual. She brushed her teeth while simultaneously making a pot of coffee. The aroma of the warm roasted beans overpowered the room as she filled her mug, reminding her that any odors would soon be eliminated by the first puff of her cigarette.

It was cool enough outside on an early April morning that her feet still needed the comfort of cotton socks as a layer of protection. For a few minutes, Amelia dug through her dresser drawers, but inevitably chose the bright blue pair with rubber grips. Despite being covered in giant holes, the socks were a robotic decision with no chance of becoming overwhelmed. A small victory.

She sat on the edge of her bed and slipped one foot into each sock. Her frail arms were barely able to push herself up to a standing position. A sea of white stars flushed over her vision, making the room spin. Three days without eating could do that. The grips on the bottom of her socks were the only thing that would keep her from losing her balance walking across the hardwood floor.

Amelia opened the door to her balcony, holding a book in one hand and her pack of cigarettes in the other. She sat on the cold, metal rocking chair and took the first seemingly rewarding, yet unfulfilling drag as the white stick sizzled between her fingers. After reading a few pages and finishing her first smoke of the day, she mentally checked off the boxes as complete. Onto the next task.

She took Luna for her morning walk and brought her back home for breakfast. One cup of generic dog food scooped into her bowl. Amelia sat in her blue suede chair at the head of the kitchen table while Luna ate so she could write. The start of another mundane week.

Miranda insisted she create a routine, which she did, but it never lasted.

"Losing your job doesn't mean you still can't find structure in your days," Miranda's voice tickled the back of Amelia's mind right on cue. "Routine gives you purpose, meaning, direction."

Amelia's mental health was the root cause of why her previous jobs didn't work out, and this last one was no exception. She had to find new ways to occupy her days.

"Routine is one of the most important things you can do right now to..."

"To help me recover. I know, I know."

Two years ago, Amelia was diagnosed with anorexia nervosa, binge eating disorder, and bipolar II. She was officially put into a box and defined. It was her scarlet letter for the world to see, shame she wore like a badge that gave others an open invitation to look down upon her. She had always viewed herself as tainted, unworthy, and broken. Only now she had a label. She was sick.

But if she isolated herself, no one would know her dirty little secret. No one would have the chance to judge her. So, she kept to herself. It was easier that way. Just like the decisions. No decisions, no consequences. No relationships, no explanations.

Amelia opened her journal to a fresh page noted by a receipt she used as a bookmark from her latest trip to the library. She hovered her pen over the cream-colored sheet of empty lines waiting for the words to come out.

She hated most things about her body, but not her hands. Her hands were powerful. They could capture her thoughts, aspirations, or fictional stories, taking her far away from the world she knew. Writing was therapeutic, especially with a pen and paper. The permanency of inner thoughts. Once the pen hit the paper, there was no going back.

Everything from that point forward was unapologetically hers with no one there to share their opinions.

Sure, she could always use Wite-Out, but once she returned to a story, she'd see the bandage that covered something she'd once felt and experienced. She'd always know what hid behind the thick, white smear. It didn't erase her truth, just masked it with a coat of paint.

Words were her only source of intimacy, words she manifested from nothing. No matter what was happening in her life, she could dive headfirst into any world she wanted. Even if it meant there was no one there to exist within that world with her.

As quickly as people came into her life, people left. Instead, she held onto her morning routine. A cherished ritual like hunting for Easter eggs that her mom sporadically placed throughout the house. Or the classic quiche on Christmas morning, served with a side of hot chocolate and a cinnamon bun for dessert because on Christmas, per ritual, you have dessert after breakfast.

The only rituals Amelia had left were her sunrise coffee and regimented cigarette breaks. There were no egg hunts or holiday meals. Just Amelia and her eating disorder. And while Amelia thrived in the daylight, her disorder thrived in the dark.

She looked out the window towards the gray morning sky.

What's the point? It's not like anyone would read anything you have to say. You're pathetic. You're worthless. You're such a piece of shit. What do you even do all day?

The voices charged, like guns blazing, firing words of defamation and self-loathing straight between her eyes. Blood surged from the center of her chest as an overwhelming heat spread through her entire body. This wasn't supposed to happen, not on days like this.

Just breathe, Amelia.

She closed her eyes and gently rubbed her hands against the arms of the chair. It was a type of meditation Miranda had taught her.

"When you start to feel anxious or out of control, bring yourself back to the present moment," Miranda said, mimicking the same hand rubbing motion on the thighs of her denim jeans. "Say out loud what you're physically feeling. Remember, nothing bad is actually happening to you right now."

Sitting at the kitchen table, Amelia slowly massaged the ridges of the suede chair between her fingertips just like Miranda had shown her in therapy. Coarse in one direction, smooth in the other. Her breath slowed down turning seconds into minutes. She left the present and faded into the past, to a time when things were simple. Back two years ago when Amelia and Dominic were backpacking. Back to an era when she was blissfully ignorant of her eating disorder. Back to a time when accountability didn't exist.

She sat in a red leather chair with her feet comfortably propped up on a matching ottoman. The bellowing sound of a dog echoed from the bottom of the stairwell up through the cracks of the metal door, the only barrier between Amelia and the streets of Buenos Aires. The sun set gently in beautiful shades of pink and violet. A menacing falcon spread its prodigious wings to frighten its prey as the smaller birds scurried to another tree in the courtyard for safety. Through the sliding glass doors, she saw nothing but a sea of green, like a child attacking the paper with scribbles of an imaginary paradise she created in her head. This was no imaginary paradise.

The image was of a giant overgrown palm tree taking over the view from the balcony. Amelia lit a cigarette, despite having quit two years ago, never telling a soul she'd started again. She put the filter to her lips; she inhaled the smoke and the secret of her addiction remained a soft whisper lingering around her mouth. The cloud faded away into the night, never to be spoken of again. She felt the high of nicotine coursing through her blood. Her skin tickled just enough to remind herself of exactly where she was.

She was in South America.

Peeling her banana, she realized how large it was. Her taste buds had been deprived of what the world had to offer until she tasted this delectable yellow fruit from a mercado de frutas. *Her body begged for nutrition after the seven miles she'd walked throughout the blazing heat of the city. The beast of her inner eating disorder trying to make its way out.*

The vivid, challenging blend of emotions fell somewhere between fear and calm. She'd never been afraid to drink water or eat certain kinds of foods. She'd never been spooked by noises from outside, even when she lived in Tampa and knew the sounds were of gunshots too close to home.

Despite her fears of the norm, she'd never felt this type of calm before. The sweet sensation of not knowing what tomorrow brought. The relief of knowing that the only item left on her to-do list was to simply not do anything. The breath of fresh air as she exhaled every stress she had of her previous life because she finally came to a place with no time frame or set destination. She could do or not do anything she desired. It was eerie, and even daunting at times, but calm nonetheless.

She opened her eyes, bringing herself back to the present moment the meditation was supposed to cradle her in. Back to her flavorless and stagnant reality. Sitting with the memories could cause more harm than good. To think that she was only holding onto these moments because she wasn't ready to give up Dominic. The idea sickened her.

Sometimes she could look back on her days of traveling and find a sense of peace. She'd sit with the moments when she'd conquered the world beneath her callused feet, regardless of where she was in her disorders or the uncertainties life would inevitably bring. Through Miranda's meditation, she opened the vault of nostalgia and tested the waters to see if she could handle the memories.

The calm rushed out of her system. Time for another cigarette.

Amelia went outside on her balcony and sat back down on the metal rocking chair, facing downtown. She faced this way for two specific reasons.

First, it was the best view of the city from her apartment. She could see the top of the Capitol Building and the skyrise towers in downtown Denver. Second, she hoped her neighbor was looking up at her.

Every day since she moved in, a man in his thirties around Amelia's age, sat on his stoop two doors over and three levels down. She wasn't romantically drawn to this stranger. She simply wanted to feel acknowledged in this world by someone other than herself and Luna. Someone to watch out for her and have her back even when she wasn't looking. He was consistent, and Amelia needed consistency. This person was as close to a guardian angel as she'd ever get while meandering through a life of isolation.

The smell of smoke lingered as she sipped her coffee, overly saturated with hazelnut creamer. Another habit she'd developed from Dominic. She liked it though. Like drinking caffeinated chocolate milk. Coffee was a stimulant to help provide temporary energy she wasn't getting from food. It suppressed her appetite which was the perfect pair to her nicotine.

Amelia picked up her phone to mindlessly scroll through Instagram. The first post she saw was a video of some B-list, British comedian sitting in a hospital bed. Tubes were going into the crevice of his elbow and down his throat. The caption read, "I'm an anorexic and have been in recovery for eight years. Everyone needs a hobby, right?"

Real cute.

She clicked the three little dots to keep reading. Despite her annoyance, she wanted to know how he managed eight years of living instead of suffering.

"I ended up in hospital due to coffee loading. It's when you substitute food for coffee. Coffee gives you all of the energy, but none of the

12

calories of food. What you might not know is that coffee reduces your pulse rate when you don't eat because there is no fuel in your body to sustain itself. I was rushed to the hospital and placed in a room next to someone with cancer. He asked me, 'So why are you here?' I said, 'Oh... I had too much coffee.'"

An irony she resented and ignored.

That would never happen to me. I've got it under control.

She put her phone in her pocket and extinguished the cigarette she swore would be her last, just as she did every morning. Until an hour or so later when she'd be back for another. That one would be her last. And then another. That one would definitely be her last.

Amelia walked inside and hung her pink and navy sweater on the back of the leather chair to air out the smell of cigarettes. Even though she smoked, she didn't want anyone to know. It was taboo and there was nothing she hated more than providing ammunition for anyone to judge her. For something that was supposed to calm her down, smoking brought on more anxiety than she thought it was worth.

She grabbed her laptop from the kitchen bar and sat back down in the blue suede chair to try writing again. While writing by hand was therapeutic, it was also time consuming. Typing allowed every thought to find its proper flow, if her fingers could keep up with her brain. Time wasn't meant to be wasted on days like this. She anxiously raced the clock before she lost all productivity.

Thanks to the human condition and the influence of her father's workaholic nature throughout her adolescent years, Amelia believed success was measured entirely on stability, security, and building a solid career. Mix those together with two cups of mental illness, a tablespoon of a broken family, and bake at 375 degrees for approximately thirty years to taste the bittersweet hints of anxiety.

Miranda's mantra homework had Amelia telling herself the same words over and over again. That didn't mean she believed them.

"Pick a phrase you can repeat back to yourself." Miranda's voice was soothing like warm caramel dripping down your throat. "How about, *'Producing does not mean living'?*"

"That's easy for you to say," Amelia scoffed under her breath.

"Care to elaborate?"

"Look, I love my dad to death. But he doesn't play the classic parental role in my story." Amelia's cheeks were flushed; tears blurred her vision. She hated crying in front of Miranda. She felt like she needed to be strong for this person she was paying to lean on. Amelia wiped the inside corners of her eyes with her index fingers.

"Simon worked in his corner office in the living room and would only come out for dinner. I don't have many other memories of him from when I was growing up, aside from him working all the time."

Amelia did have one memory with him. They were speeding down the winding Avril Hill Road in his Jeep Wrangler. The top was down on an afternoon in July while "Crossroads" by Bone Thugs-N-Harmony blasted through the speakers. Amelia was terrified for her life at the rate he was driving, but she didn't care. She was happy. For once, she had a dad.

Simon wasn't the kind of dad she brought boyfriends home to and he'd spew a speech about respect and to have his daughter home in one piece by ten. He wasn't the kind who gave her life advice on her first day of high school to guide her towards the righteous path of making wise decisions. But in that moment, driving twenty miles over the speed limit, she had a dad and not a live-in Vice President of Operations for Lockheed Martin.

"You go to college. You get a job. And you don't stop," Amelia continued. "Now I can't even keep my shit together long enough to hold down a job. I can't imagine what he'd think of me right now."

Miranda waited to make sure Amelia was done with her thought.

"Have you told him about your eating disorder yet?"

"No...."

"Time isn't the enemy. People do actually change. Maybe it's worth telling him now."

Producing does not mean living.

Amelia slammed her laptop shut. The quiet throughout the two-bedroom apartment became overpowering. Luna, a Labrador mixed-breed with giant dark eyes, whimpered softly for attention. Amelia, happy to oblige, got up from her chair and crouched down to Luna's level. With her arms wide open, Luna nestled her head between her mother's legs for a hug. A divine Swiss Roll moment. That's what Amelia called it when Luna was wrapped up like a Little Debbie's Swiss Roll or did something as sweet as chocolate.

The pages weren't going to miraculously write themselves if she just stared at them for hours. Besides, Luna's happiness always took precedence. If Luna was happy, Amelia was happy. If Amelia was eating, Luna was eating. A perfectly weighted balance beam.

She slipped on her dirty crochet UGGs, right foot then left, and clasped her fanny pack around her size zero waist. She grabbed biodegradable poop bags, keys, and her phone. Placing her Bluetooth headphones over her greasy, unwashed head of hair, she grabbed Luna's leash and headed out the front door for another walk.

Luna picked which direction they'd go. One less decision to debilitate herself with. If Luna went straight, Amelia would follow. If Luna ran into traffic, Amelia ran into traffic. Less thinking, less anxiety, less chance of making the wrong choice she'd have to take responsibility for.

They had two options. Turning right out of the gate would take them towards Colfax and en route to the Capitol. Turning left would take them towards her guardian angel's apartment building. Luna, as the decision maker, pulled on the leash to turn left. Amelia followed suit.

Amelia hoped her mystery neighbor would be on his stoop, as grateful to see these two strangers as they would be to see him.

Chapter 2

They were only a few feet outside the front gate before Luna lunged into a sprint. She tugged on the leash in a panic, nearly yanking Amelia's arm out of its socket and throwing her off balance. Luna ran towards the mystery neighbor's stoop where he was perched on the steps smoking a cigarette, right on schedule. A small dog with pointy, crooked ears was daintily curled up in the dirt next to its owner's black and dusty Converse.

Luna stopped at the foot of the stoop, whining for Amelia to set her free. Amelia had no choice left but to introduce herself. If she didn't say anything, she'd forever be known as the awkward lady with her spastic dog who passively strolled by every day. She wanted to be more than the casual neighbor who'd moved onto their shared block two weeks ago. He could be her friend, one without any preconceived notion of who she was in her previous life.

Amelia cleared her throat to get his attention. Not that Luna leaping towards him like a lion ready to pounce on its prey hadn't already done so.

"Hey…" Amelia said with hesitation. "I see you almost every time I walk by this building and haven't said hello yet."

She froze, unsure what to say next.

Was that too creepy? Do I sound like a stalker?

Her palms were getting progressively sweatier. She rubbed them against the light gray sweatpants she hadn't changed out of in two days.

"So…I guess this is me saying hello! I'm Amelia, and this is Luna."

A cartoon-like smile beamed beneath her neighbor's squished nose. His voice was chipper, more so than she'd anticipated.

"Hello! I'm Emmett, but everyone calls me Stoop Kid. And this is Kerrin." He pointed to his sleeping dog in the dirt.

Emmett. His real name. Not just a fictitious character she created in her head and dubbed as her guardian angel. He was a real human being with a real name she could put to the face. He had an identity. Emmett.

He wore a grayish-green newsboy cap above his mullet, faded skinny jeans, and a red checkered flannel shirt with the sleeves rolled up his forearms. Rectangular black frames rested on the bridge of his nose, the lenses clouded and filthy. Kerrin popped up from her slumber and frantically licked his face. Probably the reason for his smudged glasses.

"Stoop Kid, huh? Like that kid in the show *Hey Arnold!*, right? But have you ever actually left the stoop?"

"Only a few have ever witnessed it. To most, I simply manifested here. I *am* the stoop. Hence, Stoop Kid."

Amelia liked the way he talked. There was something poetic about it, like a true Renaissance man.

"There are two rules of the stoop," Emmett continued before Amelia had a chance to fumble over what to say next.

"Rule number one. Treat everyone like a human being. Rule number two. Don't die."

"Seems easy enough," Amelia replied. "I think I can manage those."

"Would you and Luna like to sit with us on the stoop?"

Amelia panicked. She hadn't planned for this. She hadn't prepared herself for the off chance she'd actually have to sit through the anxiety of a social situation. She needed to find an excuse, something she never fell short of.

"I need to take Luna for a walk, but if you and Kerrin would like to join you're both more than welcome."

What are you doing!? Why did you offer to let him come with you? Of course he's going to say no because no one likes you. You don't have anything to say so even if he says yes, you'll wander the streets with him in silence and be reminded for the next twenty minutes of how little you have to offer anyone.

Her interior voices began to settle into their usual place, chiming in at the most inconvenient times. But that's what they did. They preyed upon her when she was vulnerable.

"Kerrin gets a little finicky after her morning walk. She more than likely won't be up for another one right now, but how about tomorrow afternoon?"

"That sounds great," replied Amelia, lying through her teeth. The social anxiety permeated through her neck and into her ears. She rubbed the left lobe with one hand to calm herself down while trying to wrangle her energetic pup with the other.

"Luna and I live on the other side of the Molly Brown House. It's gated with enough grass and shade for the dogs to play. Maybe we can hang out there?"

The Molly Brown House was a highlight of the neighborhood. A Queen Anne architectural monument of bricks on top of bricks. Lion sculptures guarded the front steps with purple and green flags waving in the air. There were walking tours throughout the home of the infamous Margaret Brown—also known as "The Unsinkable Molly Brown"—who encouraged the crew of Lifeboat Number Six of the sinking *Titanic* to return to the wreckage and save other survivors. They never made it back to the ship, despite her best efforts.

It seemed fitting for Amelia to live next door. A woman of perseverance who continued to be a philanthropist and advocate for social justice throughout the early 1900's, even when people refused to listen to her. Amelia wanted to be as strong of a woman as Molly Brown.

Having the house in plain sight through every window of her apartment was a constant reminder of the type of person, the type of woman, she wanted to become.

Emmett took the last drag of his cigarette and tossed it into a tall ashtray standing next to the front door.

"We'll see you both tomorrow then!" He seemed enthusiastic about their puppy playdate.

Maybe he actually wants to hang out with me instead of feeling obligated to.

Amelia nodded at Emmett in agreement. She put her headphones back on and continued walking. By shielding him from the radiation of her socially stunted shame, Emmett could hold onto the untainted view of her for one more day.

She counted their interaction as two small victories. One for actually starting a conversation with a complete stranger and one more for making plans. All she had to do was stick to them. But there was already an excuse lingering on the tip of her tongue just in case she needed to bail out at the last second.

To aid in the reconstruction of her emotional and mental strength, she performed daily practices of gratitude. She kept track of her small, yet powerful accomplishments, forcing her to recognize moments that deserved an applause. A gratitude journal seemed petty at first, but Amelia was desperate. She was willing to try anything if it meant getting her life back.

Each triumph held their own unique power over her disorders. A task as small as taking a shower or a feat as big as introducing herself to a potential new friend, these were her successes. They were achieved by Amelia and Amelia alone, even when the voices tried their hardest to claim their victory.

The two girls walked up a few more blocks before Luna turned right onto 11th Street. She made another left back onto Pennsylvania Street, heading towards home. Amelia dangled a stick above Luna's head. The dog jumped into the air like a kangaroo on her hind legs in order to snatch it from Amelia's hand. Big Tuna's jaw fell wide open with the dopiest of smiles. Her wet tongue drooped over the edge of her elated mouth.

Luna Bean. Tuna. Tuna Bean. Big Tuna. Luna Berry. Looney Tunes. Lunatic. She had countless nicknames, but her formal name was Wheezy Luna Cita. Wheezy because she always had a slight wheeze in her tired breath. Cita, because Amelia loved everything about the Latin culture, and she was, in fact, her little moon.

They made their way through the front gate, up the stairs, and back into their apartment. Amelia replaced her lukewarm, overly creamed coffee with room temperature water. Staying hydrated was essential. The body signals the feeling of hunger to the brain if it's dehydrated. If she was hungry, she drank more water. On the flip side, drinking too much water made her bloated. While it was temporary, water weight was still an added number she couldn't bring herself to see on the scale.

It was already late afternoon and she still hadn't eaten. Day three without food. A record since her last bout of food deprivation. The entire experience was a competition with herself. How long she could hold out without eating would then be rewarded with the skewed notion of having control over her body after years of it being lost to others.

Amelia had eaten breakfast once since she'd moved in, lunch maybe three times. Her routine used to consist of making an omelet after her daily jog and shower. A period of time when she took care of herself. Her mother, Gwen, was a master in the kitchen. She taught Amelia what she claimed to be the right way to cook an omelet: eggs, whatever cheese was in the fridge, garlic, red onion, spinach, maybe some peppers, and of course butter. Never cooking spray, always butter. Amelia couldn't remember when she took this out of her routine, but knew subconsciously it was her little monster at it again. "Little monster"—that's what she called her eating disorder.

Miranda reiterated the importance of giving her eating disorder a personified name, but Amelia was too afraid. It was easier to refer to it as some mythical creature.

"It's about turning something hypothetical into something tangible." Miranda always spoke with her hands, but not in an aggressive way. Like she was being descriptive with her body.

"Ya, but then I'd actually have to admit to myself that something is wrong with me." Amelia held back the urge to cry. "That I'm sick."

Miranda rested her forearms on her thighs and clasped her hands together, leaning closer towards Amelia.

"Isn't that the point? Putting a face to your darkest demon to make it more real?"

A humanization of her disorder. Just like turning her mystery neighbor into the real-life Emmett.

Amelia opened the refrigerator and looked at the empty shelves and drawers filled with rotting vegetables. Another roadblock. There was nothing edible that didn't require taking a dreaded trip to the grocery store.

Three cans of albacore tuna and a fossilized stack of whole wheat wraps sat in the pantry. Most of the vegetables she'd bought almost two weeks ago had now grown a coating of mold. She'd forgotten to put the raw chicken in the freezer and it was way beyond saving at this point.

She slammed the door of the cold, taunting vessel in frustration, but the anti-slam, child-safety of the new, fancy appliance left her unsatisfied. There was no way she could get herself to the grocery store now. Amelia gained the courage once every other week to get herself past the front doors of King Soopers. She'd speed down the aisles, pay at the register, and rush back home to put the food in its proper place. That didn't necessarily mean she was going to eat any of it.

Grocery shopping was a very intentional task. The thought alone was enough to cause a panic attack, so she'd robotically purchase items from her safe-food list, another of Miranda's propositions.

"They're precautionary measures in case you're having a tough day." Miranda's voice popped into Amelia's subconscious, yet again. "Things like an emergency call list or writing down go-to restaurants for meals if you don't have the energy to cook." Amelia hadn't cooked a proper meal in weeks. "If you were to make a safe-food list, what would you put on it?"

Amelia pulled a magnetic notepad from the refrigerator. Across the top of her list she wrote "Safe Foods" in bubble letters, writing slowly and taking her time in order to procrastinate actually making the list.

Taking inventory of her fear-foods, however, was an effortless task. Anything with gluten was forbidden, pasta and bread in particular. Fried was no longer in her vocabulary. Dairy products like milk and cheese gave her a near heart attack if they were in close proximity.

Burgers were off the table. Periodically she'd treat herself to one, but only after a hike at least six miles long and with over a 1,000-foot gain in elevation. When someone acknowledged how frail she'd become, they'd insist she eat a burger, which made her resent the beefy patties even more.

The smell of pizza put her into a depression. Mostly because she loved it so much, but the delicious pie reiterated she'd be dining alone. Amelia thought of pizza as a communal experience. Eating in general felt like it was meant to be a group activity. Sitting around a table and sharing a meal with someone else was a life Amelia didn't have. Not for a long time.

What she could eat on occasion were her own skewed versions of tapas, which were essentially variations of snacks she convinced herself

23

were a full meal. She jotted down blueberries, rice cakes, and mixed nuts onto her safe-foods list, immediately adding the words NO SALT in parentheses next to the nuts. Salt made her bloated, throwing her down a cascading spiral.

The hunger pangs were getting worse. Water no longer satiated the monster, so she tended to the other one that lived inside her: the nicotine monster. She walked back over to the refrigerator and found a few stalks of celery that hadn't yet gone bad. She took a bite, letting the soggy celery linger in her mouth for a few seconds, then spit it out into a paper towel.

That'll suffice for now.

Her eating disorder didn't always look like this. There were times she found comfort in food, eating until it physically caused her pain, particularly anything with chocolate. Ice cream covered in caramel. Chocolate chip cookies. Brownies. Fill in the blank with any food made with massive amounts of processed sugar and ingredients ending in *-ose.*

The bingeing would usually start when the loneliness made an appearance. Sip after sip, bite after bite, she'd fill the void with decadent foods until she could no longer feel the emptiness, only stomach cramps.

It was well past noon, her usual time of declining productivity and any remote sense of normalcy.

Tomorrow will be different.

She couldn't wait for that moment. The one where her consciousness would become aware and her eyes would slowly open with the sun. An opportunity. A glimpse of a potential that hadn't been tainted. But like a speeding truck going down a one-way street in the wrong direction, the crash would be inevitable.

Now she was at that turning point. The harrowing moment when hours turned to minutes and minutes turned to seconds. Everything slowed down, reminding her of the isolation. A familiar kind of pain where, even with ten or twenty hands reaching out, she still fell back into its arms. Besides, there was no chance to hurt even more when she was always hurting anyway. It was just a hurt she'd gotten used to.

A bowl will do the trick.

Smoking weed alleviated the shame and guilt associated with eating, removing all of her inhibitions. It also made her lazy, unmotivated, and triggered the bingeing.

Shit, that's right. There's no food.

With no munchies in the house, Amelia put the weed back into the drawer of her nightstand and went out to the balcony for a cigarette. It was usually best to binge at night just before bed anyways. No time left in the day to dwell on her actions. Not until the morning when she'd have to deal with the repercussions of the world's worst stomachache. Her logic was to make sure she didn't eat for the entire day after a night of binging, rationalizing it as compensation.

She tried explaining this to Gwen once.

"No one seems to understand how I could possibly have a disorder where I'm obsessed with restricting food, but also force it down my throat," Amelia said to her mom over the phone.

"So then help me understand," Gwen responded, for the first time allowing Amelia the space to talk. It wasn't her mom's fault. She was Sicilian, and a talker.

"It's not about the food, or my weight, or how I look. It's about control."

Life seemed to be removed from all sense of the word. Her little monster always managed to put food at the forefront of her mind, clouding her judgement and dictating her actions.

Amelia smoked a cigarette on the balcony, facing Emmett's apartment per usual. Even with a name and identity, she still wanted to believe that he was in some way her protector, her patron saint of lonely souls.

She came back inside and locked the door. She put her right foot in front of her left, balancing on the tips of her toes to peek through the window to see if Emmett was there, but he was nowhere in sight.

A heavy blanket of defeat enveloped her. There it was, the sadness coming at her like a thick fog. Time and time again she returned to the same sheets that barricaded her from the rest of the world, blocking out the daylight to hide from reality. Sleep was her only companion. The longer she was awake, the longer she'd be reminded of her isolated existence. The more she was asleep, the less the world existed. The less she'd have to acknowledge. The heaviness caused her knees to buckle beneath her as she fell to the ground.

Please stop. Please. Just stop. Not now. Give me just one day. I promise I'll make this one different.

Amelia tried to persuade the darkness of her depression to recede. It was a barter system she only ever attempted when it was too late. She didn't know how long a depressive episode would last—sometimes only a few hours, sometimes for several days—but in that initial moment she always knew that the monster had won and there was nothing she could do about it.

She crawled on all fours into her bedroom, closed the blinds, and buried herself from head to toe under the covers of her freshly made bed. Not to sleep, because she knew there would be no such thing, but to let the rest of the day pass her by. She just laid there in a comatose fashion, shedding a tear every few hours. The sun would rise eventually, but then again, she never knew how long the dark would take over.

Chapter 3

Nausea crawled from her stomach into her throat, waking her from another restless night of broken sleep. It was an exhaustion that made her feel like Freddy Krueger would be coming down the hall into her bedroom at any moment, ready to whisk her away into the darkness along with him.

Days would go by without sleeping more than just a few hours. Hallucinations of shadows turning into monsters, but she was never afraid of them. She constantly lived with monsters far more terrifying than something under her bed or hiding in the back of her closet. Nothing was scary when she knew it was coming.

An intense, sharp pain pierced her lower back.

"Ahh," she cringed, sucking air through her clenched teeth.

Hunger was striking once again. Barely able to move, she flopped on her side to find comfort in Luna.

Amelia knew what her body needed, but her little monster had other plans. She couldn't trust what she felt in her heart or the never-ending dialogue in her head, but her body never lied.

When she was nervous, blood would rush to her face causing her cheeks to flush. Her ears would tingle and her hands would shake with tremors. When she was in danger, her heart would speed up and her palms would become clammy, indicating her fight or flight responses. When she was hungry, abrupt pains would radiate throughout her stomach and her back followed by a surge of shame. She'd hit herself in the face with disgust. Her body never lied.

That didn't mean she always listened.

An uncontrollable twitch emerged in her left thigh. She often felt a similar twitch near the stye beneath her right eyelid. But over the last few days, she'd experienced similar twitches all over her body, along with excruciating and unwelcome foot cramps. Dehydrated, stressed, and going on four days without food. A recipe for muscle spasms.

Next the vertigo kicked in. It didn't matter if she was horizontal. Her body didn't care that the room spun beneath her every time she closed her eyes. As if she were one with the earth, so in touch she could feel it turning on its axis. It was a feeling she wanted no part of. It was time to get up.

She blindly reached for her phone to check the time: 5:28 a.m.

Could be worse.

An opportune time to write. Creativity sparked at weird hours. She kept a journal on her bedside table just in case a notable thought made an impromptu appearance—and of course to record her daily victories. Amelia wasn't going to fall back asleep. Instead of lying there, she got up to write about her exhaustion and irritability.

She fought through her fatigue to rise from her pillowy prison. Rinse, wash, repeat. Her morning routine. Luna Bean was too tired to move, snuggled up under the comforter with eyes begging for her mother to come back to bed. Amelia carefully walked herself along the wall of the hallway, leaning in close in case she fell from the vertigo. She went into the kitchen and made herself a cup of coffee in preparation for her morning balcony visit. She grabbed her smokes and sat outside to watch the sunrise.

Metal bars with fleur-de-lis pointing to the sky lined her three-story high, outdoor sanctuary. The Capitol Building hovered above a five-story building with floor to ceiling windows. Amelia's balcony faced northwest, so she only ever saw the sunset. Sunrise was a special treat. At just the right time, she could see the reflection of the Colorado sunrise reflecting shades of pink and orange against the building's windows. Today was starting out with a small victory.

The incessant twitch distracted her, pulling her away from the moment. She rubbed her thigh with both of her thumbs as hard as she could, unsure if that would be enough to stop it. She planned to hydrate herself just as she did every day, but, as always, dreaded knowing that food was the only solution to her inner tremor. It didn't matter. She'd rather deal with the annoyance of bodily twitches than the humiliation of beating herself after eating, a few open hand slaps to the face as punishment for how grotesque she felt.

The view of the sunrise in the reflection wasn't as long-lasting as she thought it would be. Besides, her mind had drifted somewhere else. She picked up her smokes and headed back inside.

The last day of my twenties. What a bullshit year.

Tomorrow was Amelia's thirtieth birthday, a period of twenty-four hours she wanted to gloss right over and pretend didn't exist. With no one to spend it with or reasons to believe her life was worth celebrating, it was better to act as if tomorrow would be just another Wednesday.

She grabbed her laptop and placed herself on the sectional couch facing the fireplace. Four delicate paws slowly tapped across the hardwood floors. Luna walked over and laid her head on Amelia's lap. She stared at her mother with pathetically sweet puppy eyes, clearly waiting for Amelia to give her the signal to join her.

"Up, up!" She offered Luna a tiny space on the couch to place her warm, soft body. She jumped up and Swiss Rolled next to Amelia's thigh. Opening her laptop, Amelia started a new GoogleDoc. She placed her tired eyes on the screen and grazed her fingers across the keyboard. A blank slate for a blank mind.

She needed more coffee. The whiskey to her alcoholic nature, an anorexic's vice. She looked towards the kitchen. It was much too far for her to walk, especially with the vertigo refusing to subside. Plus, Luna looked so cozy; she didn't want to disturb her. Amelia liked feeling Luna's legs push against her. An adorable, softened yelp came from Luna's snout. She must have been dreaming of something nice, like running in a field or chasing a bird. Dreams as Amelia knew them were more like nightmares. Coffee wasn't worth disturbing Luna's dream state.

On the rare nights she could actually sleep, Amelia would be startled awake at an obscene hour bathed in a cold sweat, panicked by a dream where Dom always managed to show up. Occasionally there were dramatic fights that had him apologizing, begging her to take him back. In some dreams, he was a complete stranger; someone passing by on the street. Over time, the night terrors became less frightening and intense. She'd gotten used to them because again, nothing was scary when she saw it coming.

She stared back at the empty screen.

Four days without eating and two without writing. Maybe there is a correlation here, Amelia. Either way, you suck.

She couldn't get herself to expel a single thought, not with the twin distractions of annoying twitches and an aching stomach calling on her to eat.

Amelia glanced over at the guitar leaning up against the wall. Dominic had bought it for her back when they lived together in their first apartment outside of Aurora. Amelia woke up the morning after one of their fights and saw a Luna Electric Acoustic Guitar propped up against the kitchen table. It had a gorgeous spalted spruce veneer with moon phases as fretboard markers. There was a big red bow with a letter taped to the neck of the guitar.

I didn't do this to buy your love. I bought this for you because you deserve

30

it. I want you to play music and, every single time you pick it up, to remind yourself how amazing of a person you are.

She'd played it a few times since she got it, singing songs she wrote about her sadness. She'd sit on her balcony and softly sing to herself. It was hard to play more than one song before her fingertips started to burn. It needed new strings which she bought, but now it was just one more thing to procrastinate. Procrastination, another byproduct of depression. The empty desire to do nothing while she buried herself with belittling thoughts.

Amelia's stomach flipped upside down as she tried to hold back what was either a burp or a need to dry-heave from an empty stomach. She held her abdomen and rolled in closer to Luna, grabbing her shins in the fetal position.

Miranda would be so disappointed in me right now.

She never wanted to hurt anyone, especially the people who were only trying to help her. And why was she so concerned about disappointing someone who wasn't actually her friend?

"Every time you say no to food, you're crossing a boundary," Miranda would say. "Boundaries are difficult to set, especially because we tend to draw them in the sand. The line can be moved at any point."

"Shouldn't I be cutting myself at least a *little* bit of slack?" Amelia asked with a hint of teenage angst in her words.

"Giving yourself grace and compassion is absolutely part of the process. But you're the one who says what your boundaries are, not me." Miranda was blunt. Amelia liked that about her. She didn't beat around the bush when Amelia was acting like a child. Miranda spoke the hard truths Amelia needed to hear. Miranda pulled out a sheet of paper and drew a line across it in blue ink.

"This is the line. Imagine you've drawn it in wet cement. Eventually it will dry and become permanent. Boundaries are crucial for your recovery. They need to be acknowledged and set every day. Don't just write down the boundaries you think you 'should' have." Miranda threw her hands up in air quotes. "Write down the hard boundaries you actually want. The ones you deserve."

Every moment masked itself as an opportunity to cross the lines she'd set for herself, another test of how far she'd come. She'd conjure up one of her lingering excuses and denounce her boundaries in exchange for a brief moment of ease. She'd let this one slide, and the next, and the next. It was the domino effect, one excuse leading right into the next until she realized she was actually unhappy for not sticking to the original boundary she'd set in place.

Today was still young; there was still an opportunity to make this one different. Just like she'd told herself the day before, and the day before that. She wanted to find the strength that once existed within herself and remember that her boundaries weren't on a timer. There was no beginning or end. Amelia could reset herself and solidify her boundaries right then and there. She wanted to choose to flip the hourglass. She wanted to choose to eat.

Her phone vibrated on the coffee table. Someone was calling at six in the morning. She looked down at her phone. It was her mom, which made more sense since she lived on the east coast two hours ahead.

I don't have the mental stamina for this right now.

Gwen either wanted to check in and make sure Amelia was eating (followed by an hour-long conversation about painting the kitchen or returning her recent and unnecessary teapot purchase), or she needed to vent.

Amelia and her mother had an incredibly close relationship. It had its ups and downs, but there wasn't anything that one didn't share with the other, even if it was a difficult conversation to have. Amelia was terrible with confrontation. She assumed the end result would be her fault, causing her to resent herself before the interaction even began.

Gwen was the first person to be straightforward with Amelia about her blatant issues around conflict. She never let Amelia back down when things got tough. When they'd get into a fight or strike up a conversation that was too overwhelming, Amelia would shut down and hide in her room. Unable to sleep because of the constant worry in her head, she'd write a letter and tuck it neatly underneath the slip of Gwen's doorway so she'd find it first thing in the morning. Amelia was always more articulate with her feelings when she wrote. Gwen would come out of her bedroom after reading the letter to find Amelia in bed, approaching the subject in a new way, but never backing down from her stance.

Amelia picked up her phone to answer.

"Hey, Mom, how's it going?"

"Oh, well it's going." Her mom always had a positive outlook on life and managed to find a silver lining through laughter. Her unenthusiastic response meant this was going to be a vent session rather than a debrief on her last trip to the department store.

"What's going on?"

"Well...it's not all bad news. And I don't want you to freak out." Amelia immediately panicked. Her fight or flight senses fired off their warning. Her body never lied.

"You can't start off a conversation like that knowing I'll definitely freak out. What is it?"

"Remember when I went for my mammogram?" Of course Amelia remembered. It was six months ago. The doctor had said the image showed some calcifications that would most likely go away on their own.

"I had my follow up appointment. Turns out they found something that led to more tests. I don't want you to be alarmed, I just want you to pray for me. They said I'll have the results by the end of the week."

Amelia held her breath. Did she hear her right? If she held her breath long enough, the fear of being so far away from her mom would be overtaken by the panic from asphyxiation.

"Why didn't you tell me you went back to the doctors?"

"Amelia, I know how you can get with things like this. You already have enough on your plate. I didn't want you to worry." That was typical Gwen, not wanting to burden someone she loved. Like mother, like daughter.

"Okay, so what do we do now?"

"Now *we* wait, and *I* will do some yard work."

Gwen seemed strangely calm considering that she just delivered potentially life changing news. Amelia couldn't think about food at a time like this. She needed to give her mother every ounce of attention she deserved. She already had enough to deal with given that her husband, Peter, had onset dementia and was declining more with every passing day. Her mother would wake up at three in the morning to find that he'd disappeared, only to have the cops return him to their doorstep six hours later. It would've been selfish for Amelia to talk about her own issues, or only be half invested in a conversation with her mom. Cooking could wait. Food could wait. Amelia's feelings could wait.

"You know it's going to be okay, right Amelia?"

"I know. It has to be. You just seem so...calm."

"Nothing surprises me anymore, really. I've been alive on this planet for almost seventy years. Through four children, the divorce, and now with Peter. I'm not afraid. And you want to know why?" A brief silence filled the space between them as if she were waiting for Amelia to ask her why, even though Gwen would tell her anyways. "Because I have God on my side."

After thirty-three years together—a third of a century spent dating, in marriage, as partners and co-parents—Simon had left Gwen for a new woman, a woman with whom he'd had an affair, a woman who was now his wife. Only twelve when her dad left, Amelia hadn't been able to comprehend her mother's heartbreak.

But as she grew up, Amelia went through her own series of heartbreaks which brought her closer to her parents. Their relationship became more than mother, father, and daughter. They were friends. Best friends. Amelia hated living so far from them both, but she'd spent the majority of her life splitting herself in two. Two parents in two states on two opposite ends of the country. Living in one and visiting the other, keeping the spread of Amelia and her siblings fair and equal between their parents.

God, please don't take my mom. Not yet. I'm not ready.

Amelia rarely talked to God anymore, but she needed to plead with someone.

"Just do me a favor."

"Anything, Mom."

"Try not to worry. There's nothing we can do about it at this point."

Her eyes couldn't focus, like she was staring through walls instead of at them. Gwen went on talking about how Peter put his metal coffee thermos in the microwave again. They lightly brushed on conversations about new countertops that needed to be installed in the bathroom and how the weather down in Florida had been unbearably hot. They talked for over an hour about the most mundane things when all the while cancer might be building up inside of her breasts.

Amelia didn't want to smoke. She didn't want to eat. She just wanted to hug her mom.

Eventually Gwen bid her farewell so she could go on a walk with Peter. Amelia set her phone on the coffee table. Nauseous and now crying, she began mentally listing off her failures, making sure she didn't skip anything worth mentioning.

I'm a failure of a daughter for moving so far away. I'm a failure of a person for not immediately insisting I pack my bags and drive down to Florida. I'm a failure for not having the right words to say to my own mother when she tells me she might have cancer.

She slid off the couch and curled into a ball on the floor. Her mom, her best friend. The one who gave her life. It was never supposed to happen like this. Gwen was supposed to live to be a thousand years old, drinking wine with her mentally-sound husband. They'd sit side by side on their lanai, overlooking the lake in the backyard for decades to come. The world was completely out of Amelia's control and there was nothing she could do about it.

She wiped the tears from her face and blew her nose into her shirt. She couldn't go on like this. Standing up from the floor, she collected herself by rolling her shoulders back and taking a deep breath. She would change nothing by wallowing until her mom's results came in.

I didn't sit around all day when Dad had his scare and I'm not going to sit around and dwell on this now.

A few years ago, Simon had gone through similar tests, only his were to examine spots the doctors found in his lungs from his decades of habitual smoking. Amelia couldn't think about it too much. Then she'd have to acknowledge her own deathly habit.

It was only Tuesday. She needed to do something, anything.

Amelia wrote down a list of the exact moves she was going to make next. She'd make breakfast, take Luna for a long walk, and get back to writing before it was time to meet Emmett. Four bullet points, an amount that usually choked her up but now seemed slightly less daunting in such a format.

Emmett. How am I supposed to pretend everything's okay and act normal in front of him?

She couldn't waste time working herself up over something like that. She needed to stick to her list. Amelia opened the refrigerator and stared into the empty, cold chamber of torment. Just like that, another boundary she'd made for her little monster was broken. The shelves and drawers would remain empty and she had no intention of doing anything about it. Amelia shut the refrigerator door.

Food can wait.

Chapter 4

"There are three types of days for me," Emmett said, sitting with his legs crossed and a stick tucked behind his ear.

"Surviving, striving, and thriving. They all have their uses. Surviving days teach us what we're made of. Striving days show us where we need to go. And thriving days let us know that all our struggles, our pain, and our hurt have been worth it."

Amelia took a mental note. She needed to write that down to refer back to later. She really should've carried around a tiny notebook with her at all times for moments like these. Another mental note.

The two of them basked in the afternoon sunlight in Amelia's front yard while Luna and Kerrin continued to sniff and investigate one another. Kerrin panting with her black and white bandana tied around her neck to match her dad's, Luna stretching her white belly across the freshly cut grass.

Amelia was juggling thoughts about Gwen, the empty shelves in her refrigerator, and the paranoia that Emmet somehow already knew tomorrow was her birthday. Each thought berating the other with the hope that none of them would leak through her fake smile. She certainly wasn't going to tell him she was turning thirty. The embarrassment of how pathetic she'd be spending her birthday alone was icing on the metaphorical cake.

About a week earlier, Amelia bought herself thirteen candles spelling out the words "happy birthday." She wanted to make cupcakes and treat herself to their sugary goodness without fear of hitting herself. Maybe she'd have one day of self-compassion.

Amelia loved birthdays as long as they weren't her own. She treasured celebrating a day that brought someone she adored into existence. A person entered into this world and was now a part of her own universe. It was something worth turning into a national holiday.

A comfortable silence filled the little bubble Amelia and Emmett created for themselves. This person she'd just met was burrowing into her heart at a rapid pace, like she met him for a reason.

"I think today I'm just surviving," Amelia responded, veering her eyes towards the blade of grass she twirled between her fingers.

"I get it. I'm honestly terrified of my own self at times that I have to merely survive. I realize what I'm going through in the moment will let me know who I am and what I'm made of. And I tell myself that I've survived so much in my life, I must be made of so much good stuff by now."

Kerrin snuggled up into Emmett's armpit looking for attention, not begging for it like Luna usually did. She was Emmett's service dog and they'd been together for nine years now.

Emmett was diagnosed with schizoaffective disorder as a teenager. He went through six months of electroconvulsive therapy. Haunted by hallucinations of demons, he finally made a profound and brave decision. One day, en route to a corner coffee shop, he felt one of the demons following close behind. He came to a halt, whipped around, and asked the demon flat out what it wanted. Turns out, all it wanted was to dance. So, in the middle of the sidewalk in broad daylight, Emmett began to literally dance with the demon that was so very real to him and so very invisible to everyone passing by.

"I turn towards my demons and dance because they're the only ones with the answers I need." Emmett spoke so earnestly to Amelia, his words seemed to ignite.

"Resilience." She meant to say it in her head, but the word slipped between her lips.

"Precisely." Emmett smiled, exposing his teeth that were covered with a slight film from years of heavy chain smoking much like her own.

She was loving their conversation more than anything she'd done in a long time. He was easy to talk to. Their connection felt special, different. They'd already spent hours sitting in her front yard sharing their backstories—where they were from, how they got here, and about their deepest insecurities. She didn't have to pretend to be someone she wasn't. Emmett understood what it meant to suffer in the darkness of mental illness, and to come out the other side thriving.

They could be as deep as they needed to and not have to fear overwhelming the other, or as silly and shallow as speaking in Russian accents while making up bizarre, funny scenarios. Emmett rolled his cigarettes by hand and tried to teach Amelia how to roll her own. After the second failed attempt, she passed the rolling papers and tobacco back to Emmett.

"No sense in wasting anymore."

"I got you." Emmett rolled a perfectly clean cigarette and handed it to her. "For the lady."

For once Amelia didn't feel self-conscious about being bad at something. Being in the presence of someone who didn't belittle her was such a new experience. It meant everything to her.

There weren't many people in Amelia's inner circle. A few were still around from earlier chapters of her life, those who were able to withstand the storms she brought upon them. The minute she opened up about her writing as her only means of consistency and purpose, she knew Emmett was instantly becoming one of those people.

"Writing and being a so-called artist are the two things that make up my entire life," Emmett professed. "My last book was initially so long my publisher had to shorten it by at least a third. I never have the problem of not finding enough words, but rather of always having too many."

"You wrote a book?" Amelia was impressed.

"I did." Emmett was humbled.

"I'd love to read it sometime."

He shot to his feet and pointed his index finger toward the sky.

"Hold that thought."

Leaving Kerrin behind, Emmett ran back to his apartment, and returned a few minutes later, waving a copy of his book in the air.

"I had a bunch of these in case I needed to send any online orders. This one is now yours for the keeping."

Emmett handed her a four-hundred-page, soft cover copy of his life story. Amelia wanted to cry. A complete stranger giving her the best almost-birthday gift she could've asked for and he didn't even know it. She wanted to learn about his life, and now she could learn about it from start to finish in the most vulnerable and intimate way possible.

"Are you sure? I can pay you for it." She couldn't. She barely had enough money to pay for her hypothetical groceries. The whole unemployed thing.

Emmett waved his hand in a nonchalant, no-big-deal kind of way.

"It's nothing. If anything, it's kind of nerve wracking. People have ugly and embarrassing layers. And one of the reasons I'm nervous for you to read my book is because it shows so many of mine. But I also know I wouldn't be who I am without those aspects of myself. And since I'm 100% human, I know that's probably also the case with everyone else.

"My book is a direct product of my biggest failure. But having written it doesn't make me a success. I get to define success however I want or need to and being a quality human who treats others well is what makes me a success. I have a strong feeling you're also a quality human being who treats others well. Which makes you a success. Doubly so since I get the impression that other people don't treat you as well as you treat them."

Amelia was stunned. An eloquent monologue summarizing a kind of success she'd always wanted to believe. Emmett saw her for exactly who she was and didn't run in the opposite direction.

"Happy Birthday to me," Amelia sang under her breath—another internalized thought escaping via her slippery tongue.

"Wait, it's your birthday?"

Shit.

"Tomorrow is." Amelia fumbled her hand rolled cigarette and dropped it on the ground.

"Well happy early birthday, Amelia! You're going to have to see me tomorrow so I can give you a proper gift."

"No, really, you don't have to. Your book is more than enough. It's kind of a weird time for me so I'm not really celebrating it anyways." She was too nervous to share that she'd bought sad and lonely candles for herself to put on top of a sad and lonely batch of cupcakes.

But Emmett insisted. They exchanged phone numbers so they could plan to meet up for a walk with the dogs the following day.

Amelia didn't know if the words that were about to come out of her mouth next would be a mistake or not. Either way, the comfort she found in their conversation was enough for her to pull the trigger.

"Why are you being so nice to me?"

Emmett looked at Amelia with endearing eyes.

"One of my delusions is that I believe I'm being monitored at all times. I accept it as a fact and cannot convince myself otherwise.

"But I also know how ridiculous and unlikely it is. Or like my hallucinations—I experience them as part of reality, but I also know that no one else can see them."

Amelia didn't understand, which Emmett must have read by the look on her face.

"What I'm saying is that you, Amelia, are real. You are 100% human just like me. You are *not* some contradictory belief or conspiracy. You are valid and deserve to be treated as such by every person you allow to enter into your life."

Her heart beat faster and her armpits began to sweat profusely. It wasn't out of fear or anxiety this time. It was pure and innocent adoration for another human being. Someone who saw her and had her back, even when she wasn't looking. Her guardian angel, her patron saint of lonely souls.

"Would it be okay if I hugged you?" Amelia asked. She didn't realize she'd started to cry. Without saying a word, Emmett smiled and opened his arms for a hug. She hadn't experienced physical touch from another person in months. It was warm and comforting, even with his slightly pungent body odor from sitting in the heat wearing a long sleeve flannel. Amelia didn't care.

She dried the tears from her cheeks with the back of her hand. Amelia looked down at her phone in the grass to check the time. They'd been sitting outside long enough to get burnt from the Denver sun. The Mile High City. One mile closer to the sky.

"I think I'm going to head inside before my translucent skin starts to fry. Thank you again, Emmett, so much." If Amelia had to choose one quality about herself that she liked, it would be her sincerity.

"Anytime," Emmett said, going in for another hug to say goodbye. "Here is the first of your daily reminders that you're a wonderful human being."

Amelia pulled back to show her gratitude with a smile. She pulled out her keys, unlocked the main door, and let Luna take the lead up the stairs to the third floor.

The minute she entered her apartment, the world decelerated around her. Everything moved in slow motion again, like a sloth attempting to make its way across a branch. Within seconds of being alone, the little monster had suppressed every ounce of positivity she'd just experienced. She wanted to fast forward to the part where she'd be asleep again, away from her lonely world.

She looked down at Emmett's book sitting on the counter. The cover showed a young man's face wearing sunglasses. Clearly it wasn't Emmett, but rather some stock photo his publisher had chosen. It didn't match his anarchist vibe or depict the shaggy mullet he had prior to moving on his corner of Capitol Hill over seven years ago. He'd said he hated the picture, but Amelia loved it. It was a portal into his world. A world other than her own that she could dive into as a distraction. What better time to start reading it than now?

There was a tinfoil-covered bread pan on the counter next to Emmett's book. Amelia lifted the foil, exposing an entire loaf of banana bread. She'd forgotten that she'd made it a few days ago. It was still fresh, as proven by the waft of the decadent pastry taunting her nostrils. She'd baked it with good intentions, but like her groceries, she'd never gotten around to eating it.

Amelia grabbed her bowl and packed it with whatever weed she had left.

If only my neighbors knew my true reason for smoking.

Some of the residents of her building attached a stigma to smoking weed despite it being legal in Colorado. Maybe it was generational. Retired couples shot glares of harsh judgement in her direction when she walked by. The looks made her self-conscious and indicated that they didn't like her.

Her neighbors didn't know she got high because she wanted to give herself a break from the constant, self-induced pressure. They didn't know she was only trying to calm her anxiety and allow her body to finally eat. People tend to judge what they don't know. They create their own narratives instead of reading directly from the source. She'd have to stealthily smoke her bowl in the corner of her balcony, basking in the shame that triggered her need to smoke in the first place. All she wanted was to pretend the little monster didn't exist and take a bite of her homemade banana bread. She wanted to feel normal. She wanted to eat.

One hit, two hits, three hits, four. She found herself on the bathroom floor. It was a poem she recited to herself whenever she hung out with Mary Jane. It took Amelia about four hits before she would grow faint and be unable to walk. She'd crawl from the balcony, down the hall, and into the bathroom which connected to her bedroom. The dizziness may have been from low blood sugar, the altitude, or a combination of both. Regardless, it didn't stop her from enjoying the high.

Each inhale swam through her like a fish through the ocean. Her breath elevated with the sensation of floating above herself. There it was. The release of shame evaporated along with any care for what others might have thought about her. All of it was now a cloud of smoke making its way through the city streets of downtown Denver. Her only concern now was to make it from the balcony to the bathroom.

Amelia propped herself up from the chair. She put all one hundred and ten pounds of her body weight onto the frame of the doorway and successfully made it inside. She dropped to the ground on all fours and crawled like a drunken child into her bathroom, collapsing against the floor to let her tired, foggy head rest on the cool tile.

The lights above the sink hummed as she stared at the ceiling. She wiggled out of her oversized sweatpants and baggy T-shirt, wearing only a pair of light purple underwear and a knitted maroon tank top she bought in Mar del Plata, Argentina. The weed kicked in and did its job, taking her away from reality once more. Her lifeless legs melted to the floor while Amelia melted into a memory. Her vision faded to white. She was back in South America, laying on the beach.

The sand was beautiful shades of white, the water far from clear. The heat from the sun had made the ocean lukewarm, like unrefreshing bath water. If she walked far enough along the coast, it would lead her to a desolate area to relax. Mar del Plata was something else entirely. The water lacked transparency and the sand burned her feet. It wasn't specifically the beach that made it special; it was the people.

From every pier were contagious rhythms of reggaeton and salsa while the lifeguards blew their whistles. There were several moments where the entire beach became a symphony of hands clapping to a steady beat. It was like everyone there spoke the same cryptic language—a universal camaraderie—and Dominic and Amelia were the outsiders. Someone nearby noticed their confusion and told them they were signaling that a child had been found and needed to be returned to its family. If a family was missing a child, they would know where to go.

Old men wandered the beach, shouting in hoarse voices, "Cerveza! Aqua! Coca fría!" *Each one was in a uniform of white, baggy pants and a Coca-Cola T-shirt while carrying coolers around their necks. Men with the darkest skin she'd ever seen toted towers of hats and suitcases filled with watches and silver chains. Women with the smoothest complexion wore plastic billboards with poorly taped photos portraying various beaded hair designs while they roamed the beach selling their craft to young ladies.*

The beachgoers themselves were a sight like no other. People of all shapes and sizes lathered their peeling skin with oils and Vaseline, as if begging the sun to give them more. The women's stomachs hung over their bikini lines, each one telling a story of their childbearing years. Amelia wished she could love the story of her body like those women.

She watched a little boy in bright yellow swim shorts run in and out of the water. Over and over again he ran back to his family on the beach, gasping for air. Drool fell down his chest. He grabbed a bottle of water, took a sip, swished it around his mouth, and spit it onto the sand. After a few more swigs, he ran right back into the monstrous waves, begging for more.

He came back again, as if on a schedule. This time he poured the water directly into his eyes. He was having so much fun. He didn't care about the repercussions of his actions.

Amelia sunk her heels into the sand to exfoliate her dry, cracking soles, worn from miles of walking in the wrong shoes. Her feet were shriveled and peeling from overexposure to the sun. But, just like the scrawny boy in the yellow shorts, she didn't care about the repercussions of her actions.

A message graffitied onto the concrete along one of the piers: "La tierra no es tu basura." Which meant: "The Earth is not your garbage." Ironically, the sand was covered in cigarette butts, scraps of plastic, and bits of half-eaten food. One giant pile of basura and no one gave two shits about it.

It was too hot to continue sitting on the towel. Amelia jumped up and carefully stepped around the sea of people to cool off in the water, despite knowing that others would see her in a bathing suit. She was okay, though. They were strangers she knew she'd never see again.

A chill ran up her body as the waves crashed against her stomach, a stomach she had forgotten about. Little by little, she walked in up to her chest and eventually dove all the way in. She brushed her hair, salty and wet, away from her face. She stood up to look out towards Dominic. Behind her, a wave was getting ready to break. It was as if, as a child, she'd never learned the lesson to not put her back against the waves.

The resulting crash sent her tumbling forward and sucked her under. It was silent down below; she wondered if she wanted to put up a fight to reach the top. Saltwater shot straight up her nose as she struggled to breathe. Finally free of the undertow, she stood up in shock and gasped for air, scrambling to make sure her lady bits hadn't fallen out.

She looked up and once again saw Dominic. Only this time he was laughing. Salty, sandy snot dripped down her face and she burst into laughter with him. They were both laughing. Together.

These were the moments she lived for. Simplistic and happy. Not a care in the world. No acknowledgment of her body or thoughts of self-hatred. Just happy.

They sat back down on their trash-covered towels to dry off with very little space between them and the next family over in every direction. The boy in the yellow shorts came back. He grabbed his bottle of water, took a black garbage bag, and set it meticulously on the sand to use as a seat. This time he drank his water, admitting defeat.

Amelia opened her eyes, a small, temporary smirk on her face. Her head still, she scanned the room until she realized where she was: Laying on the floor, admitting her own defeat. The smirk vanished, thankfully along with the dizziness.

"Slowly," she said out loud for no one to hear. She needed to remind herself to make gradual movements, otherwise she'd end up right back on the ground. She grabbed the edge of the bathroom counter with both hands and used whatever strength she had left to stand up. She blinked her dry eyes to clear them up, but it wasn't helping. Unable to see, she took out her contacts and replaced them with glasses. Amelia cleaned the lenses with her shirt and looked up, catching her reflection in the mirror.

There was only one mirror she was allowed to use in the apartment. Its sole purpose was to make sure there was nothing on her face before leaving the house. If it ever became too much, she'd use tacks to pin pillowcases or bedsheets to the wall and cover as much of the glass as possible.

She looked herself up and down in the mirror, seeing her body grow in front of her eyes. Her thighs and calves blew up like someone inflating an air mattress. There, hanging beneath her biceps, were gallons of goop, sagging and swaying in slow motion as she lifted her arms above her head. Her body dysmorphia was taking over, only allowing Amelia to see a version of herself that wasn't actually there.

"It's not real, it's your brain playing tricks on you," she said out loud, calling out her eating disorder just like Miranda told her to do. "What you are seeing is not real. It's happening because the monster thinks you're weak. It's just your brain. It's not real. That is not your body."

She repeated this mantra over and over until she couldn't take it anymore. Amelia veered her gaze away and looked down towards the floor. It was better to focus on her feet. Luna laid down on the bath rug in her usual Swiss Roll position. Luna wasn't fazed by what had just transpired. It was a regular occurrence. A part of the routine.

Amelia grabbed her phone to text Emmett and tell him what happened—the tragically comedic irony that she almost passed out in her screwed-up attempt to eat banana bread. But she wouldn't. Texting him would reinforce the narrative that she was a constant burden to others around her. She'd just met him and was already wanting to purge her hardships onto someone else. This was one of those situations where she'd let destiny take its course. She wanted to believe they were instantly connected on some spiritual level. That telepathically, Emmett knew when she was in distress and needed a friend.

Her phone vibrated and lit up on the bathroom counter. She squinted at the screen, pulling her phone slightly away from her face to make out what it said.

It was a text from Emmett. Destiny taking its course. She managed to conjure enough energy to move her fingers across the screen to respond. Too much weed and not enough banana bread. He replied instantaneously.

EMMETT: You doing okay?

AMELIA: Ya, I'm alright now, it's just one of the scarier parts about living alone. I'm good though.

EMMETT: I feel you on that. I tried to teach Kerrin the Heimlich, but she still doesn't have the hang of it.

He had this way of taking darkness and turning it into light. Probably because he had years of practice with his own demons. He'd learned the valuable skill of being able to turn something scary into something almost laughable.

Amelia set her phone down on her bedside table and went into the kitchen to grab Emmett's book. She was at ease and it was all because of a simple gesture, a text, from a near-stranger. Amelia crawled into bed and called out for Luna to join her. She sprinted up onto the bed and plopped herself down by Amelia's feet. Amelia read until her eyes could no longer stay open, allowing her body to finally sleep. Another small victory.

Chapter 5

When Amelia was younger, maybe five or six, she asked her mom a question on their way to the grocery store while she bounced in the backseat listening to "Africa" by Toto. "Mom, why isn't there music playing in the background of life all the time like it does in the movies?"

"I used to ask your grandma the same question when I was your age."

"I wish there was music all the time."

That day, Amelia's mom bought her a portable discman and the soundtrack to *Grease*.

It wasn't until she met Emmett that her reality had a soundtrack. Thoughts of him were like a montage in an indie film. Two best friends gallivanting through the neighborhood while the soft sounds of Peter Gabriel or Billie Holiday played in the background to narrate every feeling. She didn't want to get too ahead of herself. They'd only just met. But when she looked at Emmett, she saw a glimpse of hope. A piece of herself that came out the other end of all this, thriving.

Luna laid her head on Amelia's thigh, stretched out like a sloppy sausage. Amelia caressed her back as she expanded her body in the most rewarding stretch known to existence. Luna was everything to Amelia. Her comfort, her companion, her savior. Amelia didn't claim her, on the contrary, Luna marked her territory the moment they met by peeing all over her teal blue jumper. It was kismet.

Once again, it was time for her morning routine. She blindly reached for her glasses, keeping her eyes shut, not ready to face the sunlight just yet. She put them on her face and rolled over to give Luna one more delicious snuggle.

Amelia got up, made the bed, went into the bathroom, and brushed her teeth. Floss, mouthwash, contacts. Into the kitchen to make coffee. Off to the balcony for a smoke. Out into the city for Luna's morning walk. Back home to feed Tuna Bean. Return to the balcony for cigarette number two. Rinse, wash, repeat. There was, however, something different about the day. It was Amelia's birthday.

She held the coffee cup with her fingers laced around the handle. Not too hot, just warm enough to sip the local roast through her lips without burning her tongue. She watched the city's buildings wake up with the sunrise as average Janes and Joes started their workday. Windows blinked with office lights turning on, as if the world was saying it was still revolving, still moving, never stopping for anyone, not even for Amelia.

I'm thirty.

This wasn't how she imagined thirty to look. Alone with a dog in Denver. No family or friends around. No familiarity to fall back on—except for her eating disorder, depression, and manic states of impulsivity.

In high school, Amelia was assigned a project for her English class. Each student had to write a letter to themselves for when they turned thirty. She'd kept it at her mom's house, just in case she ever wanted to revisit it. But each time she read the letter, she was more disappointed than the last. The picture she'd painted for her future self was never anything like her present.

Younger Amelia asked her future self how life working as an editor at a magazine in New York City was like. Sixteen-year-old Amelia wanted to know how her marriage was going and if there was talk about having kids soon. She hoped there was a plan for children and building a house. A life twenty-seven-year-old Amelia undeniably believed she'd have with Dominic.

Amelia scoffed at herself.

I put in so much work...made so much progress. Then he leaves and it all comes crumbling down.

It pained her to think about relapsing. She had removed the people from her life that aided in her setbacks. She finished the lease of the apartment that reminded her every day of being abandoned and lied to. She even quit smoking for three months and started an extremely regimented routine. She was ready to start the next chapter and do it completely on her own.

Miranda often tried to shift Amelia's perspective when it came to being alone. "Think of this as an opportunity."

Amelia knew therapists were supposed to be helpful, but sometimes she wanted to sit with being pissed off.

"Being alone doesn't have to be the end of the world. It doesn't have to be a permanent means of living. Being alone could mean not having to appease anyone but yourself. It could mean the potential for rediscovering your creativity. Alone doesn't have to mean isolation. It could mean solitude."

Although few and far between, these glimpses of clarity and self-love raised her high above the inner demons. Amelia could escape them and see with her own two eyes that she was more than the voices were telling her. As her fragile self continued to deteriorate, these moments would become shorter and shorter.

Just survive these next twenty-four hours. You'll see Miranda less than a day from now. You've got this.

Therapy Thursdays were every other week. She paid out of pocket since she lost her job. If she could afford to continue therapy, maybe she could blossom and be healthy again. Healthy meant happy, and happy meant she'd have the ability to live, not just survive.

At least I get to see Emmett today.

Like a telepathic force, Amelia looked down towards the sidewalk and saw Emmett standing there, looking up towards her balcony at seven in the morning, smoking his cigarette. He waved and said hello. Amelia waved and said hello back.

"Would you like to come downstairs?" Emmett shouted from below. "I have a gift for you."

Amelia was overly concerned about waking her neighbors so she took a drag of her cigarette and put her index finger up to indicate that she'd be right down. Luna voraciously whined with excitement to see her new friend. The two girls went outside to welcome Emmett and Kerrin at the front gate so the dogs and their parents could walk around the neighborhood.

Emmett extended his arms in an open invitation for a hug and Amelia graciously accepted.

"Happy Birthday, Amelia." He handed her a cardboard box that had been colored with markers to look like a monster. At first she thought it was supposed to be a crude joke since she told Emmett about calling her eating disorder her "little monster." But the longer she stared at it, the more she saw how much it looked like a character from one of her favorite movies as a kid.

When she was five, her mom would take Amelia on weekly trips to the local video rental store, the only one in their small town of Brookline on the southern border of New Hampshire. Each time, Amelia would return her VHS copy of *The Pagemaster* into the slot, walk inside, and grab another copy of the same movie for the millionth time. It was a ritual that had been long forgotten.

"I know what you're thinking, it's a work of art." Emmett's remark made Amelia laugh. "But I figured since you and I both have our own monsters, I could repurpose this old, recycled cardboard box that used to hold coffee grounds. Now your monster isn't as scary, maybe it's even kind of cute. And it smells like a dark roast from Costa Rica, so that's a bonus."

She liked this notion better than creating a fictitious story about an ulterior motive Emmett certainly didn't have. Amelia named her new little monster Horror, her favorite character from her favorite childhood movie.

"Thank you," Amelia responded, cradling the newest cardboard addition to her family.

"You're welcome. Have you by chance started reading my book?"

"I have. I started reading it last night and couldn't stop until I fell asleep. I actually managed to sleep through the night. Props to you for help with that."

"Ya, I figured it was boring enough to put someone to sleep. That's why I gave it to you. I knew you were having trouble and realized my novel was just what the doctor ordered."

"No way." Amelia refused to let him talk about his work like that. "I feel like I'm studying you. Like I'm discovering you in a way I haven't done with anyone else. I wish I could learn about every human in my life this way, but I know it doesn't work like that. That's why this is so special to me." She looked down towards her cardboard monster. "Why *you* are so special to me."

He didn't seem like the type to be at a loss for words, but Amelia had managed to say something that caught him off guard. She was pleased with herself. Making a published author and wordsmith speechless, even if it was momentary. Another small victory.

"Yeah? I'm glad I get to learn more about the girl who serenades the neighborhood from her balcony."

"Say what?" Amelia's nerves kicked in.

"I've walked by your house a million times over the last seven years, and it wasn't until you moved in that I started to hear music. So I'd walk

Kerrin by your place and you'd be there, singing quietly to yourself, but I could still hear you if I tried hard enough. The Beach Boys, right?"

"Ya, that's right." She had a soft spot for The Beach Boys. "Fun, Fun, Fun" was Amelia and her dad's song when she was growing up.

It was her first time feeling embarrassed in front of Emmett. Her music wasn't something she typically shared with other people. At the same time, she realized that they both recognized the other before they even met.

"I'm excited to get to know you," said Emmett. "You don't seem like a one-layer cake either. Or even a three tier. Or whatever is the maximum number of tiers one is legally allowed to have on a cake. Be whatever kind of cake you want, today and for always. Birthday cake, red velvet, chocolate, whatever."

Her cup was overflowing. Amelia didn't need permission from anyone to be a red velvet cake if that's what she desired. Emmett only reaffirmed that she hadn't been giving herself the permission she needed.

"I think today I'll be a red velvet cake. Mostly because I haven't had cake in two years and red velvet sounds amazing." She wasn't lying. Food really did sound appealing to her. It was a complex far deeper than that.

The four of them started on a long walk around the neighborhood. They walked down 14th Street and cut across onto Emmerson, pretending to be old people wreaking havoc amongst the retirement homes. Amelia opened up about Gwen's biopsy and what that might mean for her future. Emmett confided in Amelia about how he didn't want children because he never wanted to pass down his mental illness. They bantered about nothing and everything all at once. It was all so normal. She could finally talk to someone other than her therapist and not have to articulate exactly what it meant to be depressed. For once, she could just be instead of feeling the constant need to be better.

"Do you think it'll ever get better? Growing up with heads like ours?" Amelia wasn't sure if what she said was offensive or not, but he didn't seem to mind either way.

"It's absolutely going to get better. Might get worse before it does, but it always gets better. I know it from experience."

"I really hope so. I feel like every day I fall even deeper into it. You know, the dark. No matter what I do, I just keep sinking lower."

Emmett pulled out a bag of tobacco from his pocket and rolled a cigarette while they walked. Amelia couldn't imagine multitasking like that.

"Long term, it's going to. Things will feel like we're at the very bottom of the well. But like my therapist says, 'Life is a beautiful suffering, and you'll make beautiful things with it.'"

Amelia didn't know what to say. She got flustered when she started feeling like a burden.

"Listen," Emmett continued, sensing she was speaking negatively to her inner self. "I have faith in you. You'll find dignity in your suffering and you will indeed make beautiful things with it."

She had but only one response.

"I'm really happy I met you, Emmett."

"Me too."

They turned the corner of 13th and Pennsylvania and arrived at Emmett's stoop. He invited Amelia in for one more hug before they parted ways.

"Here is your second of many daily reminders that you're a wonderful human being," he said.

"You're wonderful, too. Thank you again for the gift."

Amelia called on Luna to follow her home, Horror in one hand and Luna's leash in the other. It was already a better birthday than the last.

On her twenty-ninth birthday, Dominic took her to a speakeasy. A quaint little ice cream shop called Frozen Matter was the front for a hidden bar you could only get to if the attendants would let you into the freezer. Retrograde, the name of the speakeasy beyond the frigid doors, served artisanal handcrafted cocktails at way too high a price. Images of space and astronauts flying into the great big beyond flashed across the multiple television screens hanging on the walls.

The gesture was kind but was another clear indication that Dom didn't know her at all. Amelia loved hidden gems like that. But on her birthday, all she wanted was to have quality time with him, not to spend an entire night listening to Dominic chat up the bartender about hiking in Peru and driving across the country. He bragged about their life of travel prior to living in Denver, alluding to the resentment he still held towards Amelia for taking the nomadic life away from him.

This year, Emmett gave her exactly what she wanted. A chance to make a moment about herself, even if it didn't necessarily look pretty. She was able to vent.

Emmett taught her the difference between venting and complaining.

"Complaining is whining about something you know how to change. Venting is...having soul farts. Sometimes people need to say something over and over again until they know what to do about it."

For her birthday, he gave her a book, a handmade monster, and a valuable life lesson on soul farts. She'd take that over an artisanal cocktail any day.

Chapter 6

Amelia paced around her apartment. She bit her nails while power walking from the door to her balcony, through the dining room, straight down the hallway towards the bedroom, and back again. The bells from The Cathedral Basilica of the Immaculate Conception, two blocks away, echoed loudly enough for everyone within a mile radius to hear. On the hour, every hour.

This meant it was one o'clock. Time for nothing, because in Amelia's life, time meant nothing. She lived at home, played at home, and survived at home. The only thing time meant for her was that there were about eight hours left before she could crawl under the covers to repeat the vicious cycle. It was also a reminder that it had now been five days since she'd eaten a real meal. Back at it with the competition.

Being with Dominic brought her competitive spirit to life. Amelia didn't like to win because she'd rather cheer others on. Plus, it meant the spotlight wouldn't be on her. Dominic was born with a brain that worked in a way she'd never seen before. He went to a Montessori school in his elementary years. It was a method of teaching for students who excelled beyond what a public school could provide. The self-directed learning meant he could finish the work at his own pace—and have the rest of the time to do whatever he wanted.

In this new life they created in Denver, Dom became obsessed with fitness—a clear coping mechanism for his addiction with opioids. He worked out for at least two hours a day followed by a ten-mile bike ride. He hiked as many days of the week as he could, but only if the trail was more than eight miles long.

Dom gave her grief if she didn't at least try to follow suit, despite her eating disorder. In his eyes, no one was ever smart enough, clever enough, fast enough, funny enough, good enough. Amelia wasn't enough. He was constantly sizing her up against a fabricated character she couldn't compete against.

This wasn't a trait he was necessarily born with, but the genetics of an addict rang true within him. He spent years of his life wandering the earth in a fog, snorting lines of pills through his nose and into his bloodstream. But being an addict didn't mean six months or even two years sober and a person was miraculously cured. Like Amelia's eating disorders, it was about management and daily practice.

There was always the possibility of him relapsing after they got back to the United States. What she didn't know was that he would translate his manipulative tactics from seeking drugs onto "improving" her.

Leila had to work harder to prove her worth and value to him. If she wasn't up to Dominic's standards, she'd lose him. It was a tale he told her time and time again, always having one foot out the door.

Their last fight was a testament to that.

"I'm selfish, Amelia," Dominic yelled, throwing his arms into the air. "I don't want you to get better for yourself. I want you to get better because it will make my life *easier*." He prolonged the word more than Amelia felt comfortable with.

Easier? Because I'm too difficult to love as I am?

He planted seeds in her to ensure she'd always do whatever it took to make him happy, even if that meant internalizing her thoughts. Amelia had to be someone she wasn't—and try to become someone she could never amount to since the bar was set too high for any person to reach. It stared her right in the face, yet she didn't take his painful words as a sign to leave. She took them as a reason to get better. To be better.

The church bells chimed again, indicating it was time for Amelia to do something, anything to take her mind off of her insistent need to pace. She checked everything off of her to-do list. Clean the dishes. Do her laundry. Make sure Luna didn't die. Spend time with her new friend.

April 23 marked thirty years of living on planet Earth. A quintessential milestone for people who've reached the end of their outlandish twenties. Amelia had assumed she'd be drinking beachside with strangers from other countries she'd met at a hostel, having them sing "*Cumpleaños Feliz*" in Central America. She wanted to stop reliving her past travel experiences and create new ones.

Instead, she was home alone with Luna pacing her apartment. She got a video call from her sister and nieces living far on the other end of the country. They made brownies with candles on top and sang to her. She was the recipient of quick, obligatory check-ins from her parents who cordially shared their sentiments. All that was left was for her to make her birthday wish.

She wished she could teleport and suddenly appear in Gwen's kitchen, wearing a sequined dress ready to tear up the town. She wished she could move mountains and part seas to bring the ones she loved closer to her.

Amelia walked into her bedroom and opened the drawer of her nightstand to pull out her weed. All she found was her journal and a few pens. She forgot that she'd smoked the last of it the day before. Another thing she loved about the beautiful state of Colorado, where recreational marijuana was like going to CVS or ordering at Chipotle. She could get exactly what she wanted from a menu of items, slowly scanning the aisles of different strains, equipment, and edibles—like staring at jewelry behind a glass case without the sparkle and shine.

She grabbed her necessary belongings and left for the dispensary, only a five-minute walk from her apartment. A birthday treat for herself. For $23.61, she could legally buy an eighth of a hybrid and be back at home, smoking in fifteen to twenty minutes tops. It was so much different than having to do an illicit drug deal with a brother of a friend of a friend in high school.

Five minutes later, she was standing at the front desk, handing her I.D. to the man at the counter. He said, "Thank you," without acknowledging it was her birthday.

He obviously didn't look hard enough.

Only a certain number of people could be inside of a dispensary at once, so Amelia quietly sat in the waiting room with her palms on her lap, feet uncontrollably tapping the floor until her name was called.

Within a few minutes, they shouted her name and Amelia made her purchase of Super Sour Alien flower. She was welcomed home by Lunatic licking her feet.

"It's like you haven't seen me in months!" Amelia said to Luna in a high pitch voice only meant for dogs and babies. Even when Amelia was gone for twenty minutes, Luna always gave her one of those big hellos where her entire body wiggled. Unconditional love from a canine, regardless of how terrible of a human she made herself out to be.

She packed herself a bowl in the kitchen, brought it to the balcony, and took a hit, filling her lungs to maximum capacity.

One hit, two hits, three hits, four. She found herself on the bathroom floor. The usual song and dance.

Her clouded state of mind made her want to be wrapped up in something warm. She decided to treat herself to a long bath. It was her birthday after all. She walked back inside and made her way into the bathroom. A little bit of Epsom salt, hot water, and Mary Jane would knock her off of her anxiety pedestal. She got in the tub and averted her eyes from the mirror to ensure there was no chance of seeing her naked body. Pulling her knees into her chest, she watched the water slowly rise to the tub's edge.

Her hair was wrapped in a bun, barely held together by a broken clip. She reached back and untangled her mess of a mane, letting her hair slowly fall down and brush against her back. The heat of the water held her like a blanket. She slid down and immersed herself. Her chest, then her shoulders, then her neck, until finally she held her breath and allowed her head to fall beneath her reflection.

She was light and small, protected by the water's embrace. The muted silence of the water pressure pushed against her ear drums. She wondered if this is what it felt like to be dead. A perfect state of nothingness. In the water, she felt like she was in her own living Purgatory. Nothing good, nothing bad. Just...nothing. Enough of nothing in someone's life could make them go insane. Amelia was used to the nothingness. Maybe she could get used to living in Purgatory, or the northwest.

She believed in God but was certain that if He had to choose between her going to Heaven or Hell, He'd certainly send her to the latter. She wasn't good enough to be in Heaven. She wasn't deserving of someplace so perfect. She was a terrible Christian. She never went to church and lied to her family about her weekly attendance to appease them. All she ever did was write the occasional letter to God, asking Him for something or sharing her opinions on things she knew there'd be no response.

"Weed feels like it activates a part of my mind I don't always use or have the ability to access," Amelia said, talking out loud to God as if he was a tangible presence in the room. "It's freedom, like I'm on a staycation from the darkness. Why is weed such a bad thing?"

She didn't necessarily know for sure that you weren't allowed to smoke weed as a Christian. She just assumed not, but had never double checked. She didn't care enough to do the research. Amelia let out a deep exhale and let herself sink lower into the bathtub.

Her towel laid on the floor next to the tub so she could dry off her hands and use her phone to play music. Bon Iver was the first band that came to mind, one of her absolute favorites. They came out with a new album—titled *i,i*—in August of 2019. The fact that she didn't know this information until eight months later meant she'd stopped caring about the music she was once so passionate about. The young child in her that used to want music playing constantly in the background of life was gone, hopefully not forever.

She pushed play on the album and placed her phone next to her resting head. The acoustics in the bathroom gave the feeling of a live concert. She twirled the ends of her hair beneath the water. Her arms floated as deadweights. Her ears were submerged, only her face skimmed above the surface so she could breathe. Her lungs inhaled slowly and her chest rose to the surface. Tiny bubbles like soft pellets burst against the skin underneath her arms. She pretended she was in the ocean, surrounded by a deep and mystical underwater world. Just when she couldn't breathe in anymore, she counted to four, and slowly exhaled. Her arms and chest sank to the bottom. Inhale. Bubbles lightly circumnavigated her biceps and forearms. Exhale. Down to the bottom she went.

Thirty minutes of deep breathing flew by. The water was no longer hot; barely lukewarm. Her fingers and toes were pruned like she'd aged forty years in less than an hour. Amelia never thought she'd live long enough to experience what it was like to be old.

Her eating disorder was the world's slowest form of suicide. Her body would eventually take over, and she'd be whisked away into whatever came next—Hell, Purgatory, pure blackness without any stream of consciousness. She sank her body back beneath the water so she could experience the feeling of nothingness, the feeling of death, one more time.

She released the drain on the tub and stood to dry herself off, wondering what she'd do next. If she stayed home any longer, she'd find herself doing something stupid. Instead, she decided to take a reprieve and go to Cheesman Park.

It was the place to go during the springtime near Capitol Hill. Eighty-one acres of open fields for the cool folks of Denver to congregate. The park was always filled with people enjoying the sunshine, which meant there'd be ample opportunities for inspiration towards her next story. It was also a great excuse to force Amelia out of the house. The park was close enough that if anxiety took over, she could walk back home.

It took her fifteen minutes by foot to get there. The farther she walked, the more calories she'd burn. She walked outside the gate, up 12th Street about twenty blocks, and entered the park.

Friends gathered around with their picnic blankets and beers, listening to music, and laughing about not being able to do a headstand. Cheerleaders from the local high school practiced their routines while their moms applauded and took photos to post on their Instagram stories. Children fell off of their scooters and bicycles, rubbing the dirt off of their knees and getting back up to fall yet again.

Amelia took out her queen-sized floral sheet and laid it on the grass. She wore her bathing suit underneath her clothes just in case she could muster the courage to be exposed, letting the sun make her fair skin less pasty and transparent. But she couldn't. Not this time. Still, the intention was there. She gave herself an opportunity to be comfortable with her body, but it wasn't going to happen. One small, baby step at a time. Like when she eventually had to buy a new pair of pants.

Throughout her eating disorder, her weight fluctuated dramatically. When she restricted her food, her clothes would no longer fit, causing her pants to fall from her waistline. When she went through a series of binges, her size would jump up in a matter of weeks. She couldn't remember the last time she'd purchased new clothes. Even mentioning the idea brought her to tears. She was disgusted with herself, but she couldn't wear the same pair of sweatpants day in and day out.

After backpacking for a year, minimalism had become a part of her lifestyle, of her existence. She found comfort in her Marie Kondo-esque desire to remove any material items that wouldn't fit on her back. There was a relief in it, like she was peeling away layers of dead skin to make room for experiences rather than things. It gave her control over something.

Control. This concept of being able to manipulate the world around her, to design her own reality exactly how she wanted it to be. How could Amelia possibly believe she had control over anything? It seemed like the universe was trying to make a joke out of her. She pictured God or some energy greater than her own, laughing behind her back while she blindly searched for even the smallest amount of control.

It took almost an entire week for her to complete the arduous process of buying a pair of pants. Getting into her car, reaching the parking lot, and making her way through the automatic doors were just the first steps. Sorting through a plethora of styles and sizes to find pairs to try on was the next.

Each day she was one step closer to making the purchase. When she finally did, it was a small and humbling victory for Amelia to record in her journal. She wrote herself a permission slip to say it was okay to take the mundane things in life one incredibly small step at a time, even if that meant she wasn't ready to be out in the open for everyone at the park to see her in a bathing suit. At least she took the first step by putting it on.

Cheesman Park was unusually packed for a Wednesday afternoon. She pulled out her cigarettes and lit one to ease the panic in her chest. Smoking in public made her paranoid, but refraining from smoking made her equally as anxious.

She slipped her sunglasses from the top of her head to the bridge of her nose. They were giant pink hexagons camouflaging her into the background, like the little boy in *Big Daddy*. When the little boy was scared, he'd put on a pair of sunglasses and pretend to be invisible. With her sunglasses, she was a chameleon with giant eyeballs, able to see the world around her, but invisible to the casual passerby.

A couple sat on a large, multicolored blanket about twenty feet to her left. They sat with their legs crossed, facing each other as they relaxed from a heated game of frisbee. It appeared to be the flirtatious beginnings of a new relationship. The man took off his black baseball cap and rubbed the top of his bald head. The woman smiled tenderly at him, stole the hat from his hands, and tugged it over her long, brown ponytail. The hat was far too large, but his eyes told the story of his adoration for her by the way he looked at her flushed, red face.

They fell onto their backs and stared at the clouds, raising their arms to the sky to block the sun. Too far away for Amelia to hear what they were saying, she imagined what their story might be. Two human beings finding love and connection, the honeymoon phase when everything was simple, no knowledge of each other's baggage or the other person's history. Just that pure, innocent love when you meet someone who makes your heart race. Amelia forgot what that felt like. The couple wrestled around on the blanket until he leaned in on his right arm, held her cheek, and gently kissed her face.

Amelia looked to her right. An older gentleman, maybe sixty and wearing a white visor, walked along the trail. He spat on the ground and adjusted his sunglasses near his temples. Amelia turned around and saw a girl her age laying on her stomach, both feet swinging in the air, turning the pages of her book. A baby in the background of Amelia's scenery cried out, "Mommy!" in excitement. A puppy soaked up the sun with its owners while they ate their takeout picnic.

The world was one giant theatrical play with trillions of subplots. Amelia's was only one of the many. Every person in the world was singing a different tune, but they were all a part of the same symphony.

That didn't make the loneliness any easier.

Amelia collapsed onto her back and allowed her face to soak up the sun for just a few more moments. Winters were always harsh towards her seasonal depression, but now warmer weather played a similar role. Seeing the faces of everyone around her—friends, family, and lovers in a shared state of bliss—reminded her of everything she wanted but couldn't have.

Amelia pulled out her notebook to write a letter to God. Letters, just like the ones she slipped under her mom's bedroom door as a teenager. Maybe one day God would write back, sending a letter in the mail with His response, giving Amelia the answers to all of her life's problems in three to five business days.

She closed her eyes, took a breath, and began to write her letter to God, pleading for strength to fight through another day.

Chapter 7

Three bottles of merlot sat on the kitchen counter. Six o'clock seemed late enough in the day to have a celebratory drink.

Amelia popped the cork and poured herself a glass of wine, filling the glass all the way up to just a few centimeters below the brim. She put the glass up towards her lips. The aroma of rich plums hit just below her nose. She took the first sip, letting it coat her throat as it slid down. She rarely drank wine anymore. It reminded her too much of being in Europe with Dominic. Her body would sway from intoxication, like she was back on the boat in Prague, watching the city lights along the canal brighten as the night progressed.

But she had to forget Dom just for one more day. She needed to blur the memory for six more hours, one glass after the next until her birthday was over. Amelia grabbed her wine glass to sit in the sunroom. The sun made the room glow at certain hours, bidding a slow farewell to the day as it set behind the city's skyline.

On the coffee table were two photo albums. For Amelia, photos were more than just something to be posted on social media to gather likes for validation. She never printed them in bulk, only one or two at a time if they warranted a special place in her book of memories instead of collecting digital dust in the cloud.

Amelia picked up the top album and began flipping through each page of her collection of deserving stills. She stopped at a photo of

Dominic and her standing on top of a boulder with Machu Picchu painting the background.

Amelia slowly brushed her thumb against the photo. First her face, then trailing down towards her stomach. That stomach, that person. She didn't recognize either one. She was wearing a blue sports bra with black leggings, exposing her midriff which at the time had impeccable six-pack abs. It wasn't until the comments flooded her notifications after posting it on Instagram that the disordered thoughts began. People making remarks about how fit her body was and how great she looked. It was gasoline being poured on an already burning flame. She had to keep her figure that way.

But the reality of carrying her life on her back and hiking for multiple days at a time made her feel like she was stronger than she was, even though the truth was that she was at her weakest.

After months of hiking from Ushuaia, Argentina up to El Chaltén, Dominic and Amelia treated themselves to a weeklong stay at a bungalow in Bariloche, their final stop through Patagonia.

Whether it was the water, a dish that wasn't clean enough, or the meat they bought from the market, Amelia became unbearably sick. For two weeks, she couldn't keep anything down. She found herself around a dinner table of new friends eating raw potatoes while everyone else chowed down on delicious, homemade burgers. Eventually her appetite had shrunk to the point that she barely noticed she wasn't eating.

When they finally arrived in Cusco, Peru to begin the Salkantay Trek to Machu Picchu where the photo was taken, Amelia was only able to stomach eating every so often. At this point, the one belt they shared wouldn't fit her waist even on the smallest notch. Dom never noticed the drastic weight loss. They were attached at the hip every day so to him, it seemed gradual, healthy. She never heard a word from anyone about her body aside from the mute warnings of her wardrobe.

But that photo wasn't just about her body; it was about her state of mind. On that day, Amelia was in a cloud of bliss, extending her arms towards the sky overlooking Sacred Valley in the Andes as she rode the waves of the psychedelics Dom had given her. Before the day captured in that picture, Amelia hadn't ever tried anything like acid. Weed, alcohol, food, and cigarettes were already enough vices to keep her busy. It was always one of those things she assumed she'd never do and was perfectly content with that notion. On the third day of the trek, Dominic just so happened to have a few tabs he'd been gifted from someone at their previous hostel.

Turning away from the photo album, Amelia picked up her wine glass and took three giant gulps, leaving no drop behind. She grabbed the bottle and poured herself another full glass. Whether it was the wine or her mental exhaustion, Amelia couldn't escape falling into the well of nostalgia.

For the first hour after placing the rainbow-colored tablet under her tongue, the effects were gradual. A stillness swallowed her whole. Everything slowed down to a steady, controllable pace. Amelia wanted to swaddle herself in a blanket like a comforting suit of armor to keep her safe. But she couldn't. Amelia was deep in the jungle, miles away from the next campsite. Her words were soft; her body relaxed. The acid sharpened her vision as the mist along their morning hike grew consistently thicker.

Out of nowhere, the clouds parted, opening the trail up with a beam of light shining through the trees. She stopped abruptly and bent down, placing her hands on her thighs. Her tingling lips opened wide in astonishment. Never in her life had she witnessed a shade of green so vibrant. She froze, not wanting to move a muscle in case the vibrations of her body would make the colors disappear. She wanted to remember that moment for the rest of her life. All of her doubts, fears, and anxieties vanished. It was just Amelia and that palette of green.

After what she could've sworn was hours of aweing over the technicolored scenery, Dominic and Amelia continued on, each step taken with precision. The mist created mudslides along the path, slick beneath the soles of her sneakers. Her senses were heightened to a new and extreme level. She could see the distinct shapes of the leaves growing and taste the humidity of the jungle on her lips.

They finally made it to an opening near a set of ruins that gave a distant view of Machu Picchu. Amelia ran over to a pile of rocks, threw her backpack on the ground, and stripped off two layers of shirts. Her eyes, glossy and wide, scanned their surroundings. She wanted to feel her sweaty skin while the sun warmed her face. She didn't care that there was a group of people staring at this strange woman touching herself. Amelia was liberated.

A friend they had made along the hike had told her there was an intense energy inside of the nearby ruins. She had to feel it for herself. She ran through the passage of stone walls covered in dark green moss and was instantly shocked by something powerful, like a deep inhale pushing air against the lining of her veins. She skimmed her hands along the walls and spun around in circles. It was an energy connecting her to something, or to someone.

Amelia ran back towards the overlook and sat with her legs crossed on the grassy field. She had a sudden urge to hug Sara. Sweet, loving Sara. Her best friend of over twenty years. Her chosen sister. Amelia wanted to tell her how much she loved her and wished she could experience this with her. She called out to Sara, knowing she wouldn't hear but still hoping she could feel the embrace of Amelia's thoughts.

A buzzing sound swarmed around Amelia's head. A speedy little wasp was zooming around her shoulders. It flew into her sports bra and abruptly stung her on the top of her right breast. Amelia frantically jumped around, slapping her chest to get it out. She'd never been stung by a wasp before. The thought of potentially being allergic shot through her mind. In the middle of nowhere Peru, in potential need of an EpiPen, and she was tripping.

With a tiny prick, the wasp flew out of her bra and into the open canyon. The pain started to spread. In a clearer state of mind, the pain wouldn't have been nearly as bad. But the tingling, stinging sensation started to expand throughout the entire right side of her chest. Instead of fear or anxiety, Amelia had a profound moment of clarity. This was something she was supposed to be experiencing. She could see the fear in Dominic's eyes.

"Dom, don't worry. I'm embracing the pain. It's all a part of the experience." Amelia rolled her head around in slow circles with her eyes closed, touching her chest where the wasp had stung her. Dominic stared at her with confusion. It was the last thing he expected her to say. In that instant, she had a revelation.

There would always be a lesson behind the pain.

Amelia took a deep breath while the vision of looking down on one of the Seven Wonders of the World remained in her thoughts. Having an existential moment while tripping on psychedelics should've changed her. But it was only a temporary sanity. A short-lived moment of spiritual cleansing that never followed her home.

I could handle a wasp stinging me. I could handle carrying my life on my back across the jungle for miles.

Amelia looked down at her glass of wine.

I can't even stay sober long enough to handle looking at a damn picture.

She grabbed the glass and downed the rest, skipping right past Happy Drunk Avenue and headed straight towards Masochism Cul-de-Sac. Noises from the downstairs neighbors grew incessantly louder as the sun set. People laughing and yelling on a Wednesday evening, hanging out with their friends. Amelia wanted to be out there with them, having a beer and making jokes about something only they would know, feeling like she belonged to something, not drinking alone on her birthday.

Her social anxiety coincided with her eating which coincided with her depression which coincided with her isolation.

Dominic and Amelia's relationship wasn't healthy or beneficial for either of them, but despite the toxicity, there was still so much good she didn't want to forget.

Just one happy thought. You can find one good thought amongst the rest of the bullshit.

Thoughts of him had been tainted and only the pain stuck out towards the forefront of her mind. She sifted through the filing cabinet of her memories in search of something positive, something beautiful.

There it was, all the way in the back of the metal, mental drawer. A memory of one of their first real dates together before they left for their backpacking trip.

They sat on an abandoned stoop, drinking wine out of a can, eating ice cream, and laughing over the absolute perfection of the coffee and chocolate turtle combination they could make by sharing their different scoops. They had deep and intimate conversations over religion, expectations, raising kids. His touch was gentlemanly as he reached over to caress her face. It was soft enough to exude the respect one human should have for another, yet firm enough to reassure her that he'd be there to catch her if she fell.

These types of details—the exact flavor of ice cream or the way his hands felt against her skin—were facts she wouldn't typically remember. Her memory had been stunted due to the lack of nutrition; she was often unable to focus in the moment because she was too obsessed with food. But that delicious, memorable date was different. She didn't think of the ice cream as a caloric enemy. It was a prop in their story to accentuate the perfection of that particular evening. It added to his smile right before his lips touched hers. He leaned closer towards her ear and softly whispered the song he'd always sing to her.

"Have I told you lately that I love you?
Have I told you there's no one else above you?
Fill my heart with gladness, take away all my sadness,

Ease my troubles, that's what you do."

The way he guided her around and guarded her from the hanging trees and overgrown bushes while strangers passed them by, the eloquence in his voice, the sincerity in his eyes, the confidence in each step. In that moment, he was pure. He was everything that Amelia loved about existing in the world. A chance to feel true, genuine, love like the couple at the park.

She'd like to think that when a memory of Amelia crossed Dominic's mind that he'd think highly of her. That even if only for a brief, fleeting moment Dom could remember the way he felt when he looked back at her that night getting into his car. Not in a smitten, lustful way, but to see her as a healthy human being. Someone who wasn't at the beck and call of her disorder. Maybe knowing that Dominic's memories of her weren't tainted by the wrecking ball that was their relationship would be enough for Amelia to finally move on.

Meeting Dom was one of those things that just happened. She blinked and there they were in the middle of the Amazon trying to figure out what country to travel to next. Regardless of how many times Sara warned her it was a bad idea, Amelia put her "I'm not listening to you" headphones on and followed through with the relationship.

Taking a journey around the world with someone she loved sounded like a romantic comedy. She'd scrolled through social media looking at photos of couples traveling the globe together—a woman with her arms towards the sky standing against the background of the Bolivian Salt Flats, a man sitting on the edge of a cliff along the coast of Santorini, a couple madly, deeply in love and kissing each other in front of a waterfall in the middle of Southeast Asia. But no matter how many blogs she read, people she asked, or books she referenced, Amelia never stood a chance against what would happen behind the scenes when the camera wasn't clicking away.

I don't think this is what Emmett meant by thriving...

Screw it.

Her drunken inner dialogue continued down the road of self-destruction. She searched for her phone and started a text to send to Dominic.

AMELIA: I don't know where you are or what you're doing, but I hope that you're safe...you ducking asshole.

"Damn it, autocorrect!" Amelia shouted, deleting the last three words with her thumbs. She wanted to sound eloquent and mature, not drunk and petty.

Amelia stared at the text message. She took a deep breath and without thinking again, hit send.

She could've said more. She could've sent another text to tell him how great life was living in the city. That Luna was happy in their new home. She could reiterate to Dominic that leaving was the best thing he could've done for Amelia, but she didn't.

Six months had passed since she'd heard his voice.

"Were you ever planning on coming back from Guatemala?" Amelia had asked him during what would be their final phone conversation, her entire body shaking with every syllable. He was silent for a few seconds which should've said enough, but Dom solidified what her intuition already told her.

"No, I don't think I ever was."

She didn't know if he was going to respond to her text, reopening a dialogue that seemed unnecessary. A part of her didn't want him to, but she couldn't help that a piece of her still did. Amelia grabbed her wine and walked into her bedroom to find shelter under her covers. Regret was sinking in.

I shouldn't have done that. That was so stupid. You're weak. You're a coward. You can't handle anything on your own. All of that therapy you pay for is for nothing because you can't even listen to a single damn word of advice anyone gives you.

Miranda taught Amelia the importance of having positive conversations with herself.

"Think about someone you love," Miranda said in their last therapy session. Amelia's mind immediately went to Sara, her confidant, her soulmate. "How would you talk to them if the roles were reversed?"

"I don't know." Amelia knew. "I guess I'd say, 'Don't talk to my best friend like that.' It's what Sara always says to me." Amelia rarely spoke about her relationship with Sara in her therapy sessions. Not because she didn't love her, but because it hurt too much to think that she had lost her for so long because of Dominic.

Sara wouldn't judge her. Sure, at first she'd wonder why on Earth Amelia had reached out to Dominic in the first place, but the words that followed would be kind, gentle, and empathetic. Sara understood what it meant to be lost in a toxic, manipulative relationship—what it was like to be devalued as a human being. The only difference was that Sara had been engaged and her fiancé's choice of drug was alcohol. But no matter how empathetic hypothetical Sara would be, Amelia was still overcome by a pit of disgust in her stomach for sending that text.

Amelia stumbled over her feet and flopped on top of her bed. The pitter-patter of Luna's paws sped lightly along the wood floors. Luna jumped up, taking up more than her fair share of the bed, but Amelia didn't care. She could have the entire bed. She could have whatever she wanted. Luna was the only one in her life with zero expectations of Amelia, and for that she was always rewarded with anything she desired.

Amelia's stomach turned on itself from five days without sustenance, aside from a bottle of wine. Her sister's voice rang in her ears: "If you don't eat and get enough protein, your heart will stop, and you *will* die." Amelia needed to prevent the paranoia from sinking in any further.

Every time she went to bed without eating, she'd spend the entire night tossing and turning from the delusion that she'd never wake up. The world's slowest form of suicide. Isn't that what she wanted?

I'm not doing this today.

Amelia got up to pack herself a bowl and headed for the balcony. There was enough alcohol in her system that she knew this was a terrible idea, but she wanted to spin out. She turned to the only thing that brought her comfort: food.

A few hits of her bowl and she was back on the ground, crawling on all fours back towards the refrigerator, her eyes barely open.

"Do you see me now, God?" She laughed hysterically and rolled onto her back across the kitchen floor. She rolled back over, got on her knees, and opened the stainless steel doors. There were two frozen breakfast sandwiches she'd forgotten about. Amelia grabbed them both and stuck them in the microwave for three minutes. As she attempted to focus her disoriented eyes on the slow rotating sandwiches, she remembered her secret stash of binge snacks for moments like these.

"God, you really *do* see me!" she yelled towards the ceiling. She opened the cabinet next to the stove and pulled out a box of Oreos she'd hidden behind various pots and pans. She removed the foil from the banana bread and took a giant whiff.

Once the timer on the microwave went off, she grabbed her box of Oreos, two breakfast sandwiches, the entire pan of banana bread, and a glass of milk and went straight back into bed. Luna was still Swiss Rolled on top of the sheets, too tired to move and well aware that Amelia would be back.

It was as if she blacked out, unable to control her hands as she brought a bite towards her watering mouth. Then another, and then another. Nauseous, Amelia discovered a mound of biscuit and chocolate crumbs pouring down the front of her shirt. Only one row of the box of cookies remained and the breakfast sandwiches seemed to have disappeared. The pan of banana bread sat half demolished on her nightstand. Amelia's stomach flipped upside down, scorning her for what she'd done. A sharp pain hit her abdomen. Amelia grabbed her lower belly tightly and ran to the bathroom.

She hovered over the porcelain toilet bowl. Throwing up was never her usual eating disorder behavior. Laxatives on occasion, but never purging. She looked down at her stomach, rubbing it with the palms of her hands and wishing the tornado inside of her to stop.

She stared at the water and without thinking any further, shoved a finger down her throat. She struggled, pushing her index finger farther and farther back. She gagged, but nothing came out. Her eyes watered as she proceeded to poke at her uvula with two fingers, barely giving herself a second to catch her breath. She didn't want to give herself time to think about what she was doing. More gagging followed until she finally gave up. Her stomach wasn't going to give up the sustenance she'd just crammed down her throat. She rolled onto her back on the cold tiled floor, feeling once again like a failure.

I'm not even good at having an eating disorder.

Filled with a rage she barely had the energy for, she opened her clenched hands and slapped herself across the face, over and over again until she couldn't breathe. The same palms that tried to comfort her aching stomach were now a weapon against her.

Amelia's emaciated body folded into itself while her head dangled over her shoulder. The fight was over. She'd exhausted herself of every last ounce of energy she had left. She released her body, letting it collapse on the floor.

Chapter 8

Her frontal lobes were on fire, shooting an unbearable pain towards the back of her skull. Amelia was more hungover than she'd anticipated. Just like the boy in the ocean of Mar del Plata, never considering the repercussions of her actions until it was too late.

Amelia's body needed food—not only to survive, but to process the remains of the alcohol in her system. The thought of eating something made her sick. She could smell the wine oozing from her sweaty, salty skin.

Her throat swelled and pinched, unable to expel a sound from the hoarseness in her esophagus. The fog in her vision blurred everything her eyes attempted to focus on. She was falling apart; guilt was the only feeling that remained.

"Remember that it's not about the contents of what you eat," Miranda told her once, "but rather the emotion associated with it. You ate something, regardless of the ingredients. It's the feelings you have during a bingeing episode you need to work through."

Amelia rolled over on her side, almost hitting her head on the base of the toilet. She curled into the fetal position, holding her stomach, wishing she could've gotten herself to purge the night before.

I'm such a disgusting piece of garbage.

She was disoriented from falling asleep with her contacts in, like a layer of cement holding her eyelids captive. She grabbed onto the edge of the sink to pull herself up using the last of what little energy she had. She took out her contacts, put on her glasses, and walked over to the calendar hanging on the wall right next to the bedroom door to cross off Wednesday's date. Her birthday had come and gone. Just like that, it was another Thursday.

She looked at the big blue letters written on Friday's date. MOM'S BIOPSY RESULTS. Between her eating disorder brain and self-medicating with cheap wine, she'd forgotten about her mom. All the while Gwen was going about her days gardening, buying unnecessary household items, and pretending like nothing had changed.

But that's how she had been since she dug herself out of her own hole of depression. Gwen picked Amelia's dad up on the side of the road, hitchhiking after a long day at the beach. Simon's car broke down and he stood in the emergency lane holding a cardboard sign with the single word *please* written across it. Gwen was sixteen and Simon nineteen, just about to drop out of college in search for something more profound.

Simon went on to protest in the 1968 Resurrection City March on D.C. and the Lincoln Memorial. He helped load and unload the buses that took people back and forth from the protest sites to their camps to shower and sleep. He volunteered to set up about three thousand plywood tents next to the Reflection Pool. It had rained for days and still thousands of people showed up, trampling through ankle deep mud—SCLC Reverend Ralph Abernathy, Jesse Jackson, all of the big names of that time were there.

Gwen on the other hand went to an all-girls Catholic school and lived a very orthodox lifestyle, but still saw potential in the man with "fairy boots" who stood on the side of the road that day after the beach. She came to the United States in 1956 in the steerage of a ship called the *Roma*. They departed out of Naples, Italy and landed in New York City, eventually making it to the north end of Boston where she'd spend the next two decades. Gwen's life consisted of family, school, and then building a future with Simon.

After their divorce, Amelia's two sisters and brother moved out to start the next chapter of their lives. Meanwhile, Amelia and her mom were starting a brand new book together by moving to Florida for a fresh start they both desperately needed. It was just the two of them conquering the world together. No one else. None of her other siblings or her dad. Just Amelia and Gwen. A relationship stronger than any diamond the Earth could create. But with that also came a lot of pressure.

Only twelve-years-old, Amelia held her mother in her arms while she cried on more than one occasion. It took years before she was able to find her way out of the dark. Amelia's love for her mother was unconditional and took every word she said to heart. It could've been the reason why Amelia was so broken by a seemingly insignificant comment her mom made over fifteen years ago.

Regardless of where they lived, Gwen's bathroom was always her sanctuary. If any of Amelia's girlfriends came over, they'd always find a way to sneak into her bathroom to try out the array of makeup displayed in front of the eight-foot-tall mirrors. The steaming, high pressure shower washed away Amelia's daily sins, followed by a very specific head to toe lotion regimen. There were serums galore for Amelia's hair, which otherwise felt like a horse's tail. She could paint her nails a different color every day for the rest of her life with the amount of polish readily available in her drawers.

At an impressionable thirteen-years-old, Amelia walked into her mom's bathroom while she was getting ready for work. Every morning, she'd twine curlers through her short, black locks to keep that perfect mom-cut bounce. Amelia stood quietly next to her as she studied her mom, watching her sort through different colored powders until she found the right one to gently brush onto her beautifully aged eyelids. Mascara seemed the least intimidating of all the paints and sprays and combs, so Amelia grabbed one of her five options and began applying. Gwen looked over at Amelia with a sweet smile, watching her little girl grow up in front of her eyes.

"How are you doing, sweetie?" Gwen asked.

"I'm fine." And she was, but there was something else on her mind she had to admit. "It's just...well, I weighed myself and I don't feel really great about it. It said I'm 152 pounds."

Gwen's eyes shot open and stopped applying her eyeshadow.

"You're on your way to 160, Amelia. Don't let it get that far."

She didn't expect that to be her mom's response. Even at thirteen, she thought her mom would've said something more encouraging like, "It's just a number on a scale. You're beautiful just the way you are," or "God made you this way. He loves you, and I love you no matter what that number says." Instead, her choice of uplifting phrases was: "Don't let it get that far."

Amelia continued her morning routine of coffee and cigarettes. Reminiscing about such a pivotal moment was hard, but she knew for a fact that her mother didn't mean anything hurtful by it. She'd said so herself.

About a year ago, Amelia brought this memory up during their conversation about Amelia's initial diagnosis. Her mom couldn't remember a single detail of that event ever happening.

"I'm so sorry I ever said anything like that," Gwen had told her with sincerity. "Mothers aren't perfect you know. We make mistakes, too—just like everyone else on this planet."

And she was right. Amelia was far too accustomed to being the one making the mistakes that impacted other people. But as Amelia's younger self stood in front of the vanity mirror, she couldn't help the fact that she'd just made a subconscious decision that would impact the rest of her life.

Regardless of what was meant by her mother's words or her father's choice to create a new family, Amelia's brain had quietly planted the seed of how it would process physical beauty and emotional pain. A sponge with zero control, only human conditioning. Her sponge soaked up the nasty bacteria of the media, her parents, bullies at school who taunted her about her upper lip hair and lack of "experience." All of her learned behaviors spiraled into her teens, twenties, and eventually reached their climax at the brink of thirty.

Amelia needed to collect herself despite the hangover. She turned the knob of the shower and jumped in before the water was warm. The stream lathered her hair and trickled down from her face to her toes. She scrubbed her arms and legs as hard as she could in an attempt to remove the remnants of yesterday's mistakes, one dead skin cell at a time.

She turned off the shower and stepped out of the tub. The condensation kept the mirror covered with a thick fog so she wouldn't have to see herself. She threw on an oversized T-shirt and a pair of baggy sweatpants. Nothing tight or constricting, only clothes that would mask her body behind the cotton.

There was no stopping the sensation of stomach acid boiling up into her throat. The only thing she could do to stop the incessant discomfort was to eat something of substance. She stopped caring about the eating disorder when she was hungover. The voices in her head didn't scream at her or call her a failure. Everything was hushed by a wave of a post-intoxication.

She opened up the refrigerator and saw one avocado that hadn't managed to rot along with two end pieces of whole grain bread. No more safe or fear foods. Just sustenance. She toasted the bread and put thin slices of the avocado on top. The two pieces of toast stared at her in the face, mocking her into submission.

Amelia slowly bit into the crunchy wheat and chewed with hesitation. She could swallow it, or she could spit it out. Her first bite slid down her throat. Already the nausea was starting to subside. Amelia took another bite, and then another, until the first slice was gone. Amelia placed the plate with the second piece of toast on a shelf in the fridge for later. One small victory for the day.

Luna whined at her feet, ready to play and seize the day. The first storm of the season was getting ready to roll over the city. It was better to walk Luna now than to get caught in the rain later. Amelia didn't want to deal with a soggy dog or have to force her frail, recovering body to endure the weather. She couldn't afford to get sick on top of everything else.

Luna, per usual, ran down the stairs towards the front door. Amelia held onto the railing to keep herself from tumbling down onto her face. Out the doors and through the front gate they went, Luna pushing with her back legs to sprint towards Emmett's stoop. He sat on his usual stair with a hand rolled cigarette, wearing his newsboy cap, enjoying a mid-morning cup of coffee. He noticed the two from afar and waved at them. Amelia let go of the leash and Luna leaped onto Emmett with love and licks to the face.

"Well, isn't this the best greeting in the entire world. Good morning, Luna!" Emmett smiled from ear to ear at her adorable and enthusiastic welcome.

"Hey Emmett. How's your morning going?"

"Well, I fell asleep on the couch last night and woke up at 12:25 a.m. only to start freaking out because it was obviously Christmas and I hadn't done anything to prepare which made it incredibly difficult to go back to sleep. So that's how my morning is going."

"I'm excellent with last minute things. Need help setting up the tree?"

"I think I just might." Emmett couldn't help himself from laughing, despite his very serious demeanor. "I think we also need to sing a carol."

"I learned one when I went to Scotland if you'd like to hear it."

"I would love nothing more."

In her best, but poorly executed Scottish accent, Amelia sang the holiday carol she learned at a bar in Edinburgh. Dozens of locals had linked their arms together, screaming in unison at the top of their lungs after their fifth, sixth, seventh beer of the evening.

"It goes, 'You're a bum, you're a punk, you're an old slut on junk. Lying there almost dead on a drip in that bed, you scumbag, you maggot, you cheap lousy faggot, Happy Christmas you arse, I pray God it's our last.'"

Emmett burst out into an uncontrollable laughter. Amelia couldn't remember the last time she made someone laugh. It was unbelievably rewarding. Her brain and mouth weren't on the same page when she was hungover, which meant she had no filter. Sometimes it got her into trouble. In this case, she was on point.

Thunder clattered in the background.

"Hey, Emmett, would you like to come over and watch the storm from my balcony with us? You can bring Kerrin, too."

"I love a good rain shower. Let me run inside and grab her." Emmett extinguished his cigarette and within a few minutes came back down with Kerrin, barking and jumping towards Amelia's face with excitement.

They walked two doors down and headed upstairs into Amelia's apartment. In this circumstance, Amelia usually would've been nervous. She was having someone, a guy no less, over to her house for the first time since she'd moved in. She was barely used to having human interaction, and now she was going to be in close quarters with a man. At least she had Therapy Thursday to fall back on if she needed an excuse for him to leave.

They headed straight for the balcony and another cigarette as they watched the rain pour down.

"So this is what it looks like from up here in your tower." Emmett scoped out the scenery of Denver.

"Ya, it's pretty nice. I try not to take it for granted, but I'm only human."

"100% human if I do recall."

Emmett pulled out his tobacco and papers and rolled another cigarette. Amelia joined in by pulling out one of her American Spirits from its bright blue pack.

So it goes.

Amelia read the phrase tattooed across Emmett's knuckles. It was a line from a book by his favorite author. Amelia read multiple Kurt Vonnegut books over the last few years. Not because she wanted to, but because Dominic had insisted. It wasn't anything against Vonnegut, she actually really enjoyed some of his books. Dom just had this way of making her feel ignorant if she hadn't read the eight million books he had over the course of his lifetime. He was too smart for his own good. She never argued though. Amelia simply followed through with his suggestions because she didn't want him to think she wasn't smart.

"I think I've made a decision," Amelia said, lighting up her cigarette. "I've set a deadline for myself."

Aside from making her lists, Amelia found something definitive in creating deadlines. It provided her accountability and forced her to take action instead of remaining stagnant through her indecisiveness. Achieving goals gave her a mission. It made her a little bit lighter and able to cope until her next deadline.

"What is this deadline for?"

"Well, if June rolls around and I'm still going down this path, if I'm still not taking care of myself and am spending nights laying on the bathroom floor, I'm going into treatment."

Amelia told Emmett about passing out, wasted away like too many other nights. Too stoned to comprehend anything, buried beneath her eating behaviors. Treatment might be the only way to hold herself accountable. It would be her next mission.

Dominic suggested multiple times that Amelia should consider an inpatient treatment facility. But whenever the conversation came up, she'd fight back, telling him that treatment was for sick people. And Amelia wasn't ready to admit that she was sick. Treatment was the ultimate defeat.

Amelia compromised with Dom. If she wasn't going into treatment, she'd start going to group therapy every Saturday morning. Not only was it a way for her to connect and find support from others in similar situations, but it was also a scheduled reminder of where she never wanted to end up. Detailed stories of a woman her mother's age in the emergency room with tubes down her throat. Tears shed over friends lost to their eating disorders. Amelia didn't want to become a bag of skin and bones wilting away on a stretcher while paramedics tried to resuscitate her—or worse, wind up in a casket she'd built for herself.

"I might not see a future for myself right now, but that doesn't mean I don't want one," Amelia admitted, uncrossing her legs and folding her jacket over her chest to keep her warm. She had poor circulation because of how low her body fat ratio was, but she couldn't stop sweating because of the excessive amount of alcohol and processed sugar she'd had the night before.

Orange tinted Halloween lights were woven in and out of the balcony's barricade. They provided enough light to see the other's face, but not too much that it put the spotlight on either person. Amelia was sensitive to light and had trouble making eye contact. Too much and she'd be intimidated by the idea of someone seeing her outer flaws. Too little and she'd crawl back into herself, wondering what the other was thinking because she couldn't read their facial expressions.

Emmett didn't say anything about her considering treatment. There was no rebuttal or expression of agreement on the matter. He simply nodded his head in acknowledgement because there wasn't anything more that needed to be said. He understood and would comply with whatever she needed to do in order to succeed at becoming healthy again. Someone she barely knew had put more effort towards understanding her illnesses than someone she once thought she'd spend the rest of her life with.

Emmett's alarm on his phone went off.

"I need to take my meds," he said with a hint of discomfort. She could tell he didn't want to leave.

"No need to explain, I understand."

Amelia did understand perfectly. Eating was a series of alarms and timers. It had to be. The same meals, at the same time, every day. Otherwise she'd end up in the exact position she was in now. Emmett's medications acted in the same way. If they were slightly thrown off his days would follow suit. He was allowed a three-hour window in order to take his medications, but it was better if he kept them regulated.

Amelia walked Emmett to the front door. He rubbed Luna's belly goodbye, gave Amelia a hug, and he and Kerrin went out the door on their short, not-so-arduous journey two floors down to their apartment.

So it goes.

Alone again with only her thoughts to keep her company—and Luna of course—Amelia pulled out her phone and texted Corey for no other reason than to not be alone. She jumped far too soon into a short-term relationship with him after Dominic left. Six years older, a fixer, and set in his ways. But just like Dom, Corey couldn't handle the emotional baggage she brought along with her. Another reaffirmation that she was too sick for anyone to love.

On paper, Corey was perfect. Tall, dark, and handsome were the cliché words he used to describe himself. He had a good career, a contagious laugh, and a spirit that never let the sourness of the world taint his day-to-day life. He had a knack for knowing what Amelia was thinking. During one of her anxiety attacks at his apartment, Corey came into the bedroom and found her curled up under the covers, hiding from the glorious sunshine coming through the five-foot-high windows on a beautiful Wednesday afternoon. He laid down next to her and wrapped his arms around her frail body as tight as he could without breaking her. She never told him that this was how she was able to get through one of these episodes. To have someone hold her with a grip that squeezed every bit of panic out of her pores.

I feel safe. I feel loved. I feel comforted.

"Do you feel comfortable?" Corey whispered tenderly in her ear.

Amelia nodded her head.

"Do you feel safe and loved?"

Amelia nodded once more.

"Good."

As if her thoughts spouted through his lips, Corey said the exact right thing without any prompting.

But when Amelia moved into her new apartment in Capitol Hill, she decided that in order for her to move forward with her recovery, she needed to end her romantic relationship with Corey. If she gave herself space and time to be alone, she could learn to love herself again—to find a reason worth living instead of pouring whatever ounce of energy she had left into another human. She couldn't continue putting herself last, transferring every issue she hadn't resolved about Dominic right onto the next person.

Amelia put her phone in her pocket without sending a text to Corey. She couldn't. She didn't even want to talk to him. It was just another pathetic excuse to ease her lonely heart.

As more space and time passed between the two of them and their relationship, she realized it wasn't a temporary setback. It was a permanent detachment that broke her heart, but she couldn't ignore the red flags from those few months together anymore.

He was a workaholic, just like her dad. His inability to open up. His constant need to fix her when all she needed was someone to listen. His lack of support is what killed her the most.

In a manic episode, Amelia spewed out multiple ideas to release the pressure from her brain and Corey found a reason to squash every one of them. He needed to know the logistics of how something as insane as what came out of her mouth would ever work. She never felt supported with her ideas, regardless if they were feasible or not.

Why did it seem impossible to find someone who would cheer her on rather than snuff out her creative fire? She'd spent too many years of her life having her authentic self be squandered. She made a promise, set a boundary: she would never be with someone who would make her feel that way again. The line was drawn in the cement after Dominic and she refused to move it for anyone. Corey was no exception.

The red flags weren't Corey's fault. It wasn't necessarily anyone's fault. They were just two different types of people who had two very different love languages. Fault had nothing to do with it. Codependency, anxiety, depression, bipolar. These were all human conditions, along with a laundry list of other factors, that shaped Amelia into the woman she was. They weren't her fault.

"It's about creating new neural pathways," Miranda explained to Amelia. "You need to find ways to redesign the curves in your brain, but it takes practice."

Maybe Miranda was the answer she was looking for all along.

Chapter 9

Only one hour left until therapy. She had to make it through just one more hour and then she could be in the room with Miranda, spilling her heart out. Amelia felt as if this day was a day of striving. Emmett's voice ran through her head.

Striving days show us where we need to go.

She recognized what it took for her to get by. Drink water, walk Luna, talk to at least one other person, and eat a small meal. Nothing more, nothing less. Just enough to catch a glimpse of where she needed to go. Hopefully Miranda would shed a little light on how to make it through the darkened tunnel to get there.

Miranda wasn't her cup of tea when she first started going to therapy. Amelia had met with only one other mental health professional, but not since she was a teenager. At eighteen, she had a consultation with a male psychiatrist. Within twenty minutes of sharing her story, he cut her off and prescribed her Fluoxetine (the generic form of Prozac). One small white piece of paper with a scribbled signature on the bottom later and she was out the door. Amelia swore she'd never go back to therapy. It wasn't until hitting rock bottom that she gave it one more attempt.

Because of the lack of true care that was taken by her first psychiatrist, Amelia's assumptions of Miranda tainted their initial phone consultation. But she wanted to get healthy and wouldn't let any more excuses stand in her way. After their first session together, Amelia broke down on the living room floor of her apartment. Not because she was sad, but because she finally found hope that someone might be able to help her. It was exactly what she needed to start making strides in the right direction, a single step towards the realization that she actually was sick.

Thirty minutes left until therapy and the anxiety was already in pursuit. Miranda's office was only eight minutes from her apartment, right off Downing Street. Leaving early meant she'd have time to sit in the parking lot and write about what she wanted to cover. Her bi-weekly sessions had to be used to their maximum potential, never leaving out a single important detail.

Amelia went down to the garage, got in her car, and drove the eight minutes to Miranda's office, sitting with only the humming of the air conditioner to alleviate the silence.

She made a list of what she needed to talk about: Her recent revelation on the slowest suicide known to human existence, her recurring dreams of Dominic, her night of binge eating that broke her five-day streak, her inability to move forward. That was plenty, more than the hour would permit and enough to leave her emotionally exhausted by the end. Amelia made a mental note to leave any discussion about Emmett towards the end if time allowed it.

Four minutes left, and still nervous she'd be late even though she was sitting in the parking lot right outside the front door. She hated being late. She was prompt. Always prompt. The first to arrive at parties, meetings, or appointments, and usually the first to leave by pulling the classic 'Irish Goodbye,' fleeing the scene before anyone had a chance to notice she was gone.

One minute left. She shut the car off and headed through the main entrance. Miranda was already standing in the waiting room with her usual glowing smile and perfectly styled blond hair.

"Hey Amelia, good to see you. I'm really glad you're here."

Amelia nodded in acknowledgment. She never started talking until they were in the room together with the door shut. Miranda's office was exactly what she'd envisioned a typical therapist's office to look like. The shades were drawn and subtle lighting from two lamps on opposite ends of the room created a warm, glowing environment. A couch was placed next to her desk, comfortable but not so comfortable that someone would want to stay and call it home. Miranda pulled out her computer chair and wheeled herself in front of the couch, gesturing for Amelia to sit down.

"So how have you been?"

This is how she always started their sessions together. There was never an initial prompt to get her going. Miranda wanted to open the floor for Amelia to talk about whatever it was she needed to. It was up to her to decide where the conversation would go.

"Well, I certainly don't feel like I'm progressing at all. Digressing if anything."

"Why do you think that is?"

"Because regardless of what I do every single day, I still find myself feeling more alone than the day before. It's like, no matter how hard I try, the depression always wins."

"Let's talk about why you're in the situation you're in now."

"You mean living by myself in a new apartment? Or why I can't for whatever stupid reason seem to get a hold of my behaviors?"

"Remember how we try to talk about ourselves." Miranda always managed to put Amelia in check. "Tell me about your living situation and why you chose it."

"Well, I moved to a neighborhood that was closer to downtown so I could try to make friends and actually feel like I was living in Denver instead of a deserted island. I wanted to live alone because I needed to prove to myself that I could recover without anyone's help. I wanted to

feel independent and removed from anything that involved Dominic."
Amelia looked around the room as if the answers would appear on the
walls. "I think that about covers it."

Miranda turned towards her desk and wrote something down. She
didn't usually write during their sessions, making Amelia wonder what
she had said to provoke her to do so.

"And why do you feel like you haven't accomplished those things
yet?"

"I don't know, maybe because I'm lonely and feel like I'll never be
enough for anyone."

Miranda had a special power. Her insight, whether it made Amelia
upset or not, was never anything Earth shattering. They were things
Amelia already knew about herself and the way her brain processed
information or emotions. Miranda's power was simple. She helped her
dust off the tools she'd once had and reminded her how to use them in
their proper manner.

Miranda continued her stream of thought, "So, you wanted to be
alone, and now you feel lonely. Do you think it's possible to have
both? To be with other people while you continue working on your
recovery?"

Amelia was perplexed. Recovery seemed black and white, as if she
had to be entirely alone so as to not risk losing herself into the arms of
another person. The idea of someone as a companion had seemed out
of the question. No one would be able to complement her, like blue
and orange or red and green, colors that are perfect the way they are,
but when they're put together, they bring out something beautiful in
the other you wouldn't have noticed otherwise. Someone who exudes
beauty while standing alone, only to accentuate the other instead of
replacing.

"No, I don't think that's possible."

Miranda looked up at Amelia with a half-smile, not in a condescending way but as if she were about to bring a world of wisdom into Amelia's universe.

"Let's rewrite the narrative." This was one of Amelia's favorite phrases of Miranda's.

"Okay...I'm listening."

"What if you decided right now that having someone else in your life, man or woman, romantic or not, could also coincide with your recovery? What if you believed it was possible to live alone and focus on yourself, but also allow the human connection, understanding, and support of someone else?"

Amelia contemplated this in silence for a few moments.

"But what would that look like? It would just be me having to tell my story over and over again so that way people have a proper 'heads up' in case I turn into depressed Amelia or manic Amelia."

"I understand that. It's scary having to be vulnerable with someone else. What is it you fear the most when it comes to exposing yourself for who you are?"

Amelia paused and bowed her head towards the ground.

"I'm afraid that when they find out the truth about who I am, they'll leave me."

"Just like Dominic did," Miranda chimed in. All Amelia could do was nod her head like a small child getting in trouble for sticking their hand in the cookie jar before dinner. She didn't want to admit that Dominic still had control over her, regardless of how long it'd been since he left or the physical distance between them.

She couldn't stop the tears from falling. Miranda handed her a box of tissues, a warm and loving gesture, something she wasn't used to.

Amelia couldn't escape what had happened between her and Dominic. It was a haunting battle that lingered over her like a storm refusing to pass.

Last fall, Dominic and Amelia had gone through the worst turmoil of their relationship. Drunk at five in the morning after an overnight shift at work, Dominic woke her up by throwing Amelia's cell phone at her. Feeling Dominic drifting away, Amelia had turned to someone she'd casually dated years before. They reconnected over social media, and for once Amelia felt like she had control of a situation. She could manipulate the relationship without any repercussions, just like Dom had done to her. But then he found their texts and became enraged.

He threatened to take Luna away from her. The tone in his voice grew louder as he ripped photos off the wall of the life they built together, and shredded them to pieces. He lifted her cell phone above her head, reading the texts out loud to her while she cried. Dominic packed up her belongings into trash bags and threw them in the middle of the living room floor.

The event continued to escalate when Amelia saw a large kitchen knife sitting on the middle of their empty coffee table. Fearful of what he was capable of, Amelia eventually became the one who was groveling on the floor and begging him to stay.

They decided to give it one last shot. One last attempt to make their relationship work. They moved into a new apartment together in a sketchy neighborhood in which she never wanted to live. She had a strong feeling in the pit of her stomach that signing the lease was a terrible decision. Her body never lied. But Dominic convinced her while they waited outside the main office with the moving truck filled with furniture and household items they bought together.

"This will help us save money. And it's entirely yours if you and I don't work out." A notion she'd agreed upon. If they were going to live together, Amelia wanted to be the only one on the lease, that way she'd still have a roof over her head in case Dom wanted to move back home to Massachusetts. But that wasn't the case. He didn't move back to the northeast. Amelia dropped him off at the airport for his solo trip to Guatemala. Dom kissed her with reassurance that it would only be a few weeks apart, that their separation would only make them stronger, that he would be home back in her arms before she knew it.

The first week he was gone, she heard absolutely nothing. Radio silence as if he'd fallen into a blackhole or worse, as if he'd ghosted her like some jerk she met on a dating app. Not the heart of someone she'd devoted herself to for over two years.

When he finally reached out, he sounded distant—like a long lost third cousin she hadn't spoken to for decades. He was furious with her. While Amelia was having to navigate the long-distance silence, she was living in an apartment with no heat or hot water in the middle of November in a shady neighborhood that terrified her when she went outside most days. Yet he still managed to manipulate her to make her believe it was her fault.

"These are your problems, not mine. You haven't even asked how *I'm* doing. It's always about you."

This was the part of manipulation that made Dominic the conniving puppeteer in her story, formulating new ways to pry further and deeper into the emotional depths of a human being, only to find Amelia's weakest insecurities. Like a vampire sinking their teeth deep into the neck until they reached the walls of the capillaries, bursting through until they've tasted blood.

The reason as to why he chose Amelia was because she was a human being with something to give. Amelia gave Dominic the ability to work while they traveled since her freelance jobs were remote at the time. She passed along some side work to him, cutting her paycheck by a third. He instantly took Amelia's generosity for granted. He preyed on her in a way she didn't notice until they were too far along into their travels to bring it up.

The way Amelia saw it, what manipulators did and how they chose their prey, only one thing mattered: Whether or not they could tap into other people's emotions for their own benefit. Dom was gaslighting

Amelia to get what he wanted—a way out of his small, depressing hometown.

The distance grew between them. Time passed, they exchanged minimal words with each other every few weeks. They were over. They had been over, but neither one of them wanted to admit the hard truth until one day Amelia couldn't take it anymore.

"It's been six weeks, Dom. Six weeks." Amelia was fuming, barely able to keep up with her own thoughts, let alone convey them to Dominic over the phone. "I don't want to be used as your storage unit anymore. You need to get your shit out of the apartment if you're not coming back."

"Okay, I don't see how I can make that happen seeing as I'm in Guatemala." Dominic let the silence linger a little longer, "Can you at least mail me my laptop?"

Amelia hung up the phone, enraged by his proposition. For a month and a half, Amelia drank and smoked herself to sleep to ignore the fact that he left her. That she was too sick, too unhealthy, too damaged to be loved by him or by anyone. She wrote him a text message saying that she couldn't continue being left in the dark and pushed aside just to twiddle her thumbs like a good housewife waiting for him to finally come home.

Not much to her surprise, his only response left her feeling more denied than ever.

DOMINIC: *If that's what you want.*

Her heart had been broken before, but never like this. If Dom couldn't love her for who she was, she couldn't either.

"Are you with me, Amelia?" Miranda waved her hand in front of her face, trying to bring her back to the present moment. "What are you feeling right now?"

"I'm mad. No, I'm furious…." Amelia's voice trailed off. "But I also feel broken. I don't think I have what it takes to put the pieces back together."

"I know it doesn't feel easy, but this is the place you have to go. This is where you fall in order to rise back up. Before Dominic, what was the hardest thing you had to go through?"

This was tough for Amelia. Her entire life was like walking up a steep mountain carrying hundreds of bricks on her back. Everything seemed impossible and she could barely recollect a time when things were easy.

"I guess it was when I moved to New Hampshire after college. That was probably the most difficult time of my life I can think of before now."

"And do you remember what it felt like when that part of your life became a story you told rather than a truth you were living?"

Amelia thought about those two years living in New Hampshire. She'd been engaged and too young to know what abuse looked like, a pattern she continued to repeat. In a manic state, she packed up her belongings and moved north with seventy dollars to her name. Amelia's sister came to her rescue, reminded her what she was capable of, and helped Amelia to get back on her feet.

"I do," she whispered under her breath. "I really do. But I don't remember how I got there."

"Well, this might be hard to hear, but the truth is that it won't look the same. These are different circumstances, despite how similar they may seem. You can't copy and paste the timeline only to think that if you follow these guidelines or steps that you'll magically come out the other end. This is an entirely different story. Just remember, you are the author. You can rewrite the narrative at any time. There is no expiration date."

Amelia knew she was right, but it was easier said than done. They sat in silence for a few moments while Miranda waited to see if Amelia wanted to say anything.

"So, what's the next move you're going to make?" Miranda asked. "What's one thing you will do to start rewriting?"

Amelia played with her ring, fidgeting as she searched within the filing cabinet system within her brain. There were tons of things she could do, they all just felt unattainable, but she knew what Miranda meant. She needed to make just one decision. One move that would push her forward.

"Well, I've been wanting to quit smoking for a while now and feel like every time I try, I fail. A few hours later I'm back at the store buying the next pack."

"You bring up your smoking quite a bit. Why do you think there is such shame associated with it?"

The first time Amelia quit was one of the most difficult things she'd ever done, but she managed to kick cigarettes and shape up her life for two solid years.

"Maybe because I hate myself for starting again. For having Dom influence me into thinking it was a good idea."

"How can you rephrase the part about hating yourself?"

There she was, putting her in check again.

"Okay, okay. I don't hate myself. I was vulnerable and because of that I was easily influenced to fall into old habits that used to be a crutch." Amelia said back sarcastically. "It's a lesson learned, and still a lesson failed."

"It's not a lesson failed. But I'm going to tell you something that I want you to take some time to sit with."

Here we go, another mantra or something.

Amelia became defensive when she knew Miranda was right.

"Cigarettes." Miranda took a brief pause to reiterate the importance of what she was about to say next as she leaned closer to Amelia. "Cigarettes. Don't. Make. You. Skinny."

"I don't think..." Amelia stopped talking. Of course she thought this, every single day. The only reason she'd started smoking again was to prove something to Dominic.

"Do you think I'm pretty?" Amelia's need for words of affirmation as her love language prompted her to ask Dominic this after a few months of dating.

"Obviously I do. Do I think that there are people more attractive than you? Ya. I mean, I know I'm not the most handsome guy in the world and you probably look at other guys all the time, just like I look at other girls."

That was the same night she lit her first cigarette in two years. Dominic was anxious, looking around at other people smoking at the bar in Vienna, Austria while he pulled at his vape, clearly wishing it were a cigarette. Amelia was also anxiously scanning the room with her eyes, only she was busy comparing herself to the beautiful European women at the bar she now assumed Dominic was admiring. She couldn't take sitting with the pain of his hurtful words anymore.

Amelia marched over to a stranger standing near the smoking section. She pointed at his cigarette in his hand and put two fingers to her lips, miming a request to bum a smoke. The man laughed and responded, "Sure thing," in English. She put it to her lips, nerves shaking her from the inside out. The man lit her cigarette and with one puff, she was back on them. The chain reaction from the nicotine monster had started, and so did her eating disorder.

Miranda could see that Amelia was drifting somewhere again and needed to bring her back.

"Let's try to think through this together. That's what I'm here for, so you don't feel like you have to do everything alone." This was another feeling Amelia was uncertain how to navigate, someone insisting she didn't have to go through a difficult situation alone. Amelia fell silent, unsure of what she was expected to say next.

"I have an idea that I'd like for you to try. Something small, but it's something we've talked about before. Instead of looking at ways in which you can completely change the course of your life, why not start small. Why don't you try giving your eating disorder a name? Give it physical characteristics, a personality, and create something tangible you can face. That way, when you're ready, you can write a letter to it. Address it head on. Call it out on its shit and name it for what it really is."

There it was again. Having to face the demon that lived inside of her like a monster under her bed. The monster she ignored because it was easier to be at the very bottom of the well than it was to climb back up. The metaphorical rope burns along her hands would singe her skin, knowing her biggest enemy was sitting at the top waiting for her.

"I'll think about it. I'm not sure I'm ready yet."

"Amelia," Miranda paused. "You'll never be ready, and that's the scariest part for most people. They sit around and wait for a specific moment or a blinking sign above them saying that they are. But it doesn't work like that."

"I hear you, I really do. But what if I personify this illness and I still can't handle it? What if I fall even harder?"

Miranda took a deep breath and looked Amelia square in the eyes.

"You have to put the car in drive. No one's ever going to be able to get you where you want to go but yourself. Not even me. But don't forget, there is a passenger seat for a reason."

Chapter 10

I t was Friday, the end of the week. Or at least it was for the average person amped up for an adventurous weekend. For Amelia, a normal week was like running through quicksand without anyone there to pull her out.

What's normal anyways?

She sat on the balcony with Luna sleeping soundly on top of her cold, veiny feet. Luna quickly popped her head up and wiggled her nose. Emmett must have been right around the corner, either sitting on his stoop or walking nearby with Kerrin. Luna had such a love for him already that she could recognize his scent from three floors up, followed by incessant begging towards her mother to go to him.

Sure enough, the chiming of Emmett's keys hanging from his belt loop and Kerrin's chain leash came walking by on a slow four count.

"Hey Emmett," Amelia yelled down from above.

"Hello!" he hollered back with his usual chipper voice. More than likely, he'd been up since five in the morning, startled awake by a claw to the face from his cat, Kimchi.

"I'll come downstairs with Luna in just a second if you have time for an early Friday stoop hang."

"No other way I'd like to start my day."

Amelia put out her cigarette and ushered Luna inside to put on her leash. She grabbed her technicolored fanny pack and ventured downstairs. She opened the front door of her building to find a jumping and barking Kerrin on one side of the gate, Luna on the other mimicking her excitement. Luna and Kerrin had a mutual understanding. Kerrin was nine, much wiser than a two-year-old puppy like Luna. The big sister to Luna's little.

Luna always barked when Kerrin did because that's what you do with an older sibling. You look up to them and imitate their every move, even when they were qualities you shouldn't necessarily cling to. Just like Amelia as a young girl trying to be just like her older sisters—the girl who put lemon in her dark brown hair in a sad attempt to turn it blond but instead it shined bright orange from being too young to understand that brown doesn't easily turn blond. The girl who stood in the mirror beside her sister while she told Amelia about the sexiness of a little bump on a woman's belly, examining her own down to the finest detail.

"Hello there," Emmett said as he opened up his arms for a hug. They were some of the best hugs Amelia had ever gotten. Sometimes they went for a little too long, but she embraced them. She'd soak up every second she could. Hugging him meant someone was holding her.

"Hey Emmett, how's your morning going? Usual five a.m. wake-up call from Kimchi?"

"You betcha. Only this time I think she may have actually been trying to kill me. She might be an assassin. Who's to say?" Emmett patted the fresh wound on the bridge of his nose with his middle finger.

They walked back over towards his stoop and sat down to smoke a cigarette. The dogs found their own perfect spots. Kerrin curled up in the dirt next to the stoop, Luna at the top stair guarding the front door.

"So, I did something I can't stop thinking about."

"What do you mean?" Luna paced around Emmett, sniffing his armpit.

"You know, one of those things you do in the heat of a drunken, vulnerable moment."

"I can't drink so I have to live vicariously through other people. What did you do?"

"Don't get too excited, it wasn't one of those fun drunks. It was the kind where I make really poor decisions without thinking about what the end result might be."

"Ooo, this sounds enticing. Do tell more."

Amelia, uncertain if she should tell him or not, decided to throw caution to the wind.

"Well for starters, I texted Dom."

Emmett fell silent for a few moments. Amelia had told him all about Dominic during their first hangout in her front yard which was probably why he was taken back. He took another drag of his hand rolled cigarette. He preferred them hand rolled. Like he had created something out of nothing for him to utilize.

"And what did he say back?" Emmett's voice grew agitated.

"He didn't respond. Honestly, he probably won't. Instant regret."

Amelia could feel the energy of Emmett's discomfort turn vibrant red.

"Can I ask a question?" He averted his eyes from Amelia's, something she also did when she felt uncomfortable or nervous.

"Sure, you can ask me anything."

"Why didn't you text or call me if you needed someone?"

There it was, exactly what Amelia was afraid of. It was like she was back in the ocean of Argentina, knowing she shouldn't turn her back to the wave, but did it anyway.

"I don't know, I guess I was ashamed." Amelia's cheeks burned bright pink. Emmett was the one person she never needed to be uncomfortable around, until now.

She wanted to explain to Emmett that her choice to omit him from experiencing her vulnerable state had nothing to do with him. That it had everything to do with recovery, not just from her eating disorder, but from heartbreak.

"I just don't understand," Emmett was getting even more flustered. His speech quickened and Amelia could see his mind wander through his deviating eyes. "You can continue to obsess over someone who treated you like the scum of the Earth, but all the while I'm right here trying to be supportive of you. It leaves me feeling like I'm unworthy. Like I'm too weird, too broken, too disabled to have a relationship."

A feeling Amelia knew all too well.

"That's not fair Emmett." She tried to find the right words, knowing what she had to say next could make or break their friendship. "I'm not trying to hurt you, you have to understand that. You know I'm screwed up and I'm just trying to figure my shit out. I have issues, and you're literally the only one that knows the full extent of them. I promise this has nothing to do with you."

Emmett's entire demeanor changed. He crossed his arms against his chest and the once chipper tone felt dark and empty. He was mad, an emotion she hadn't yet seen from him.

"There is either something severely unattractive about me or else you're violating your own boundaries you've set for yourself and I need to be very concerned about your wellbeing."

Amelia's eyes widened and her head jerked back in bewilderment.

"Whoa, boundaries?"

How dare he think that he has some authority over what boundaries I set for myself.

She was torn between frustration and not wanting to lose Emmett's friendship. She could sense that her defensive reaction was not what he wanted to hear.

"You're taking this all wrong and using my own issues against me, Emmett. Can't you see that?"

"No Amelia, I'm not. I've shown you how much I care about you. All

I want to do is catch you every time you fall so that you'll never be hurt. Yet you run towards the person whose only goal *is* to hurt you."

"You know *nothing* about my relationship with Dom. Nothing." Amelia was at the point of no return. There was already such a loss of control over so much in her life, she didn't need someone she barely knew trying to control her, too. "Don't you dare try and tell me that what I did was wrong or right. It's my life and I can do whatever the hell I want with it."

Amelia threw her cigarette on the ground and stomped it out with her shoe.

"Do you have feelings for me, Amelia? I need you to be honest."

Amelia stared at the ground and slowly turned towards Emmett. Maybe she wasn't clear enough with him. Maybe she'd led him on without thinking. She couldn't ever remember saying the exact words "I don't want a relationship with you, I just want to be friends," but she did remember telling him that she didn't want to date him. Or at least she thought she did. She can't trust her memory. Only her body.

"Emmett, I'm sorry..." He didn't have to guess anymore, and she didn't have to wonder whether or not he understood. Emmett knew exactly what she meant.

"This always happens to me. I meet someone, grow feelings for them, and every time I'm confronted with rejection. I'm not going to sugarcoat this for myself. I'm sure I'll see you around with someone else at some point. Guess I'll just have to deal with that."

Amelia felt like bugs were crawling under her skin. The emotional confrontation was making her lean into her little monster, her only safe space left.

"Come on Luna, we're going home." She grabbed Luna's leash and pulled her towards the bottom of the stairs.

"That's a good idea, honestly. I think I just need some space right now."

You need space!?

She was grateful for her brain filtering out at least one thought. If someone told Amelia they wanted space, she'd give them space. She always took people for their word. It was easier than trying to read between the lines.

This was the moment Amelia had been thinking about since they met. They became everything to one another as fast as lightning, and just as fast they were nothing. Space meant only one thing, which she learned from Dom. Space meant it was over. No more front yard chats or stoop hangouts. No more Emmett, Kerrin, Amelia, and Luna. No more guardian angel.

For once, Luna was unable to keep up, falling behind Amelia's trail as she stormed back up to the apartment. The fact that Emmett, or anyone for that matter, had the audacity to tell her she was breaking her own boundaries infuriated her—as did the fact that she couldn't have him as a friend because she didn't have the same feelings as he did.

She wanted to be seen as more than an item that was meant to belong to another. She wanted to have a friendship with Emmett, one based on understanding and empathy. One that allowed for conversation and comforting. But Amelia was wrong once again.

Just like that, the little bubble they'd made for themselves had finally popped. Like everyone else in her life, he was gone. And all she could do was blame herself.

Amelia paced up and down her apartment, just as she did whenever she felt directionless. Emmett's voice played on a loop in her head.

Like I'm too disabled for a relationship.

Her anger turned instantly into sadness; frustration into self-loathing. In heightened situations her emotions could switch without warning.

She never wanted to make Emmett feel that way, or anyone for that matter. This was another reason Amelia kept to herself. If she was alone, that meant there would be no opportunity for her to hurt someone she cared about. There would be no chance she could make anyone's life worse by entering it in response to her own selfish desire to not be alone.

That was one of the reasons why she went to her group therapy on Saturdays, to find connection with others who felt just as alone and defeated as she did.

Amelia stopped pacing in a state of panic.

If tomorrow's Saturday, that means today is Friday...

The day of her mom's biopsy results. Another selfish move by none other than Amelia herself. Not a surprise. Dominic said she was selfish. She just didn't realize how selfish her disease had made her.

She jumped back and frantically scrounged around the kitchen searching for her phone, remembering she left it on the charger in her bedroom before she went to see Emmett. It was typical for her to leave the house and not bring her phone with her. It wasn't like anyone was going to call. It was a device only meant for scrolling and wishing for someone to be on the other end thinking of her.

"Siri, call Mom."

After a few rings, she answered.

"Hello, daughter, how are you?"

"Did you get the results?" Amelia completely disregarded the small talk and wanted to get straight down to business.

"I did! The doctor said it's benign, so all is good! Praise be to God!"

"Wait, that's it?" Amelia was confused. She still had a million thoughts running through her head. "Do they have to take it out? Could it get worse or become precancerous? What are the chances?"

"Amelia, slow down. It's okay, really. The doctor said there is nothing more that needs to be done. It'll be looked at every six months, but it can just sit there without any need to bother it. I can go back to life as usual."

Back to normal?

She couldn't understand how that was possible.

"Mom, that's amazing." She held back tears of relief. "How do you feel?"

"Well." She sighed into the phone. "I have to say, I feel different."

"How so? Relieved?"

"No, more than that. After he told me the results, all I could think about was you."

"Why—"

Gwen interrupted her as usual.

"Because, Amelia, it just made me reflect a lot about where I've gone and what I've done. I mean, honestly, what have I done with my life? No offense to you or your brother or sisters. I just can't help but think that I never really traveled or dreamt any bigger goals for myself. There isn't anything I can look back on and say, 'Wow, I did that.' I only ever lived for other people.

"I lived for you kids, I lived for your father. But I never really lived for me, at least not until now. And even so, I'm still taking care of Peter with his bad back. Plus his memory is only getting worse."

Amelia could hear the regret in her voice.

"I know, Mom, but like you said, you're finally living for yourself now. You're making choices to do things you actually want to do, not what you feel obligated to. And you have someone alongside you for the ride who loves you to the moon and back." Amelia's heart was breaking. She wanted to give her mother words of encouragement, just like she had for Amelia's thirty years of life. Despite whatever hardships they may have endured together, Gwen was Amelia's lifeline who had helped her through so much.

"It's what made me think of you, and your...you know, condition." She never said the words out loud. That Amelia had an eating disorder. "I want you to be healthy and happy. I want you to live your life doing the things that fulfill you. I've seen you do it before, and I know it's possible again. I just don't want you to become like me, looking down the road, almost turning seventy, wondering what you did or what you'll leave behind, thinking of all the things you didn't do or were afraid to do because of whatever reason. I want you to take care of yourself so you can live the life I never had the chance to. I want you to be free."

To be free...

Amelia thought that all she wanted was happiness and health, but the truth was smacking her in the face. All she truly wanted this entire time—through depressive spells and her eating disorder taking control—was to be free. Free of Dominic, free of depression, free of her inner demons that grabbed ahold of her neck every time she tried to breathe. She wanted freedom.

Despite hearing Gwen share in that sentiment for her daughter, Amelia still couldn't find it in her to believe she'd ever have it.

"I love you, Mom. I love you so much. Thank you for saying that. I'm so happy you're getting a second chance." Amelia meant every word. For once, she wasn't lying to appease someone. She really was ecstatic for her.

"God is filled with second chances, Amelia. You just need to have faith and turn to Him when you feel like you're losing hope."

Hope, a word filled with expectations. Her mom always turned to God through the good and the bad.

Amelia's relationship with God wasn't as strong as her mother's. Once upon a time it was, but so much had happened to make her stray. She tried going to church when she was traveling, but it was difficult when she was visiting so many countries that didn't have English-language masses. She knew the order of things so she could follow along with the motions to the best of her ability, but it made her feel distant. A stranger in a crowd of people who were supposed to be an instant community.

Dominic didn't believe in God, only science. He constantly questioned Amelia about religion causing her to doubt her own beliefs.

"God doesn't exist," Dom said to her one night at a hostel in the hills of Minca, Colombia. "And if he did, there wouldn't be such terror and bullshit happening in the world. My friends would still be alive, not dead in the ground from fentanyl."

After a few more minutes of their usual banter, Gwen and Amelia said goodbye and hung up the phone. Amelia was baffled. Why wasn't she more relieved knowing her mom was going to be okay? Because once again, her egotistical brain took a beautiful moment and twisted Gwens words. She distorted the reality of what was actually said.

What had Amelia done with her life? Not much at this point. Sure she traveled, but what had she really accomplished? Stupid job after stupid job, failed relationship after failed relationship, broken friendships, moving more times than she could count to escape a world she couldn't grasp living in.

Amelia was depressed, lethargic, hungry, but more shameful than hungry. No amount of weed could cure this beast. Everything felt meaningless. Gwen was right. She did need to get healthy and do things for herself that would make her happy.

That was the exact problem.

Nothing made her happy anymore. Nothing gave her the will to keep going. Freedom was unattainable. No matter how far into the depths of her soul she went, there was simply not enough energy left to regain control over her recovery. She couldn't achieve freedom from herself, no matter how much optimism her mom might've had.

Amelia turned back to the remains of her wine from the night before. She popped the cork and poured the rest into a giant glass, immediately opening up another bottle. Each glass turned into one more until it was time to open the third bottle. She wanted to numb the pain the only way she knew how.

Maybe this is what Mom meant by wasting my life away. Drinking and smoking my life down the drain.

Amelia wasn't working towards a goal, nor had any idea if she could ever have a job where her mental illness didn't get in the way. It was her own fault she wasn't traveling the world anymore. The person she thought she'd spend the rest of her life with ran as far away from her as possible, literally leaving the country.

She'd never find a way out.

She'd never face her illness.

She'd never love herself again.

She'd never escape her disorders.

Freedom was a joke.

Getting treatment, who am I kidding?

Getting treatment would cost her at least thirty thousand dollars out of pocket without insurance. That was out of the question. She'd never be accepted into any center if she couldn't afford it. Her last hope for recovery.

There was no point in wanting a future because Amelia didn't have one. Gwen could want it for her daughter with every ounce of her being, but it was a moot point. Even when she was able to look over the hill and catch a glimpse of the sunrise, a storm cloud brought tornados and life-threatening lightning storms to squander the view. Her depression would come through just when she was starting to think that she could find a way out. Recovery was so far out of her reach, she was done.

Her fourth glass of wine turned into a fifth as she finished the remains of the bottle. She popped the cork on the next, this time drinking directly from the source. She stumbled into her bedroom to grab a notebook from the nightstand drawer, pulled out a pen, and started to write. This time it wasn't to write a tale of a child running through the woods to find a magical swing that brought her into a different universe. It wasn't a poem about the woman she hoped to become.

It was the final chapter of her story. Her final memoir to the remaining people she thought deserved to know the truth.

She wrote her own suicide note.

Chapter 11

Her hands vibrated uncontrollably. Amelia grabbed her wrist with her left hand to try and steady its pace and allow the pen to do its final job.

Dear you,

I'm sorry I caused you pain. I'm sorry I failed you as a daughter, a sister, an aunt, a friend. I'm sorry I wasn't strong enough to make it out the other side. I just need you to know that it has nothing to do with you and everything to do with me. You're probably wondering why, and for that I want to try my best to explain. I constantly revert back to my younger self. I miss her, that radiant beam of light and joy. I miss the girl who had goals, purpose, desires, wants, drive, ambition, and freedom. I've been trying so hard to fight the war inside of my head every day and find her again. But I've realized that she no longer exists. The vessel in which I live is nothing more than a reminder of everything I once was and who I will never become. Now, all I want is to be free. Now, I can be one less burden for your heart to carry. I love you, please don't forget that.

She didn't know what more she could possibly say. There weren't enough words to condense the reality she lived every single day into a letter that would even come close to articulating what she felt. Her mom, dad, siblings, Sara. She just needed them to know she was sorry, she loved them, and it wasn't anyone's fault but her own.

All she had to show for her life were a decade of journals tainted with laundry lists of things she was going to do, but never did. Amelia was afraid of the person she was becoming, teetering over a line of destruction that would disappoint her mom's desire for Amelia to find more in this life.

She folded up the piece of paper and wrote on the back, *to you,* hung it on the fridge, and stumbled into her bathroom, carrying the remains of her wine. Amelia shut the door behind her and heard the click of the doorknob.

Crumbling down onto the familiar, cold, tiled floor of the bathroom, she laid her back against the wall with her legs spread open, deadweight in defeat. Her third bottle of merlot stood almost empty between her legs while she stared at the plastic container of her antidepressants. She was prescribed Bupropion, a drug typically meant for people who were trying to quit smoking to help ease the depressive side effects of nicotine withdrawal.

Her primary care doctor, Dr. Martin Stephens, thought this would be a good initial stepping-stone towards managing her depression. Instead, the medication made her even more anxious and paranoid. She always felt sluggish, unable to focus. Amelia had become a medicated zombie. Dr. Stephens started her on one hundred and fifty milligrams. When that didn't work, he bumped her up to three hundred milligrams, escalating the side effects.

Amelia had weaned herself off of the little white pills a few weeks prior. She'd rather feel out of control with her emotions than feel nothing at all. But the repercussions of not consulting her doctor about it threw her even further off balance. She wondered if she'd made a mistake by not taking them anymore. She'd focused even harder on her eating disorder and wasn't satisfied with the pace at which it was working. Her slow, agonizing suicide via her eating disorder wasn't happening fast enough. Her lack of eating hadn't yet shut down her heart.

Unscrewing the top of her pills, the warmth of wine coursed through her body and her eyes struggled to maintain their focus. Like a painting that was melting right before her eyes. Amelia laid out the pills on the floor, giving each one their own tile square. She locked the door so Luna wouldn't find a way to sneak in.

Amelia left Luna's dog food open and available for her to eat as she wanted; hopefully there was enough so she wouldn't go hungry. She was a ravenous, growing puppy so there was still a chance she'd eat it all in one sitting. Eventually someone would have to figure out that Amelia was gone.

She pondered the notion of her laying on the floor dead. How long would it take for someone to find her? How long would it take for someone to come check on her and take Luna? How long would Luna survive?

Her head swirled as she tried to find a focal point to bring balance back to her vision. She sank lower to the ground and sprawled out on her back with the pills beside her. It was just her and her few dozen admission tickets to the next life. She turned her head towards the door, the wine causing her to see double of everything around her. Amelia dug her fingernails into her thighs, deeper and deeper until the skin broke, releasing blood down her leg. It was as satisfying as popping a pimple. The first time Dominic saw her puncture her own thigh, he shot up from the couch and threw his hands in the air.

"I can't do this anymore," Dom said to her for the millionth time, seeing the scars along Amelia's legs. "I cook for you, I clean for you, I listen to you, I try to fix your problems, and this is what happens in return!" All Dominic ever did was treat her like a patient; all she wanted was to be loved.

"You need to do better, Amelia."

"Go be someone else's problem, Amelia."

"I'm too selfish for this, Amelia."

His voice couldn't be the last thing she heard in this life. She needed to shut him up. Amelia picked up a pill as a single tear trickled down her cheek.

This could be the end of it. This could end all of her pain and suffering. This could fix the need for one more person to destroy the Earth, take up space, and provide nothing of substance to anyone or anything. This could end her compulsions, her need to never eat and then to eat everything all at once. This little pill and its friends could end her manic episodes and her days of debilitating depression.

She grabbed a handful more and placed them in the palm of her hand. Touching each pill one by one with the tip of her finger, caressing them as if they were a tiny mouse. Ugly at first sight, but only wanting to find warmth with you if you just let them. Amelia sobbed, unable to see beyond the glaze of tears.

Did she really want to die? Did she really want it to be all over with? Of course not. Of course she wanted to have a life. She wanted to get married, have children of her own, and have a job she actually cared about. Of course she wanted to buy a house with enough land to let countless dogs roam about while she hosted weekend barbecues and birthday parties. She longed for family vacations and bonfires on the beach, to talk about life's existential questions over cheap beers. She yearned to give her parents a grandchild from her own healthy body. She wanted to have her nieces and nephews in her life playing with their cousins.

But Amelia knew better. Amelia knew that this would never come to fruition for her. Her younger self was more optimistic and more naive than she'd realized. The woman she wanted to become, the life she wanted to have, was nothing but a fairytale to be told at bedtime. And Amelia was ready to sleep.

She could hear Dom's demoralizing and passive aggressive scoff in her mind saying, "I told you so." Amelia closed her eyes and began the final countdown, starting from ten, building the courage to watch the ball drop for the last time.

Ten. *That's all it will take.*

Nine. *Only a few more seconds and it'll be over.*

Eight. *I'm making this a bigger deal in my head than it actually is.*

Seven. *Stop being a pussy and stop crying.*

Six. *Come on, Amelia. Stop shaking.*

Five. *You'll never have the life Mom wants for you. This is your only option.*

Four.

A loud, wailing bark came from outside the bathroom door. Amelia opened her left eye first, then her right as she attempted to reorient herself in the bathroom. She rolled over and put her ear to the door. Luna was crying, but not her usual puppy cry for attention. Amelia propped herself onto her forearms and stretched her hand towards the door to unlock it. Luna came rushing at her, licking her face with a force so strong it knocked Amelia back to the ground. She kept whining and crying and panting and licking. Licking like it would be the last time she'd ever get to experience Amelia's face against her tongue.

This wasn't a normal cry. This was a cry to stop. A cry for help.

Amelia exhaled deeper than she'd ever thought possible, as if she were exhaling everything she'd ever felt with that one single breath. She realized for the first time in years that she wasn't clenching the muscles of her abdomen. She folded into Luna with her arms wrapped tightly around her, weeping with fear.

"I'm sorry, baby," Amelia cried. "I'm so, so sorry I almost left you like that." She was disheveled and trembling throughout her entire body. She continued to apologize to Luna as if she could understand the words she was saying through the croaking in her throat.

Amelia shook her head in terror and shot her eyes as wide open as they could go. She cleaned up the pills, brushed them back into the bottle, closed the lid tight, and put the bottle in the back of her medicine cabinet. She crawled on all fours towards her nightstand to find her phone. She had the numbers, all she needed to do was dial.

Her thumbs scrolled through her list of contacts searching for Emmett's name. She paused and looked out at the empty room.

She couldn't call Emmett. After everything that happened, it would be just another disappointment to add to the list. She was already enough of a burden on his aching heart, she couldn't let him know that she'd almost given up entirely, that all of their talks had been for nothing.

Besides, Emmett needed space. Which was exactly what she was going to give him.

She kept scrolling through her phone, past her mom, past her sister, past Sara, and stopped at Corey's name. A person she couldn't disappoint because she'd already done so. She tapped on the screen and within two rings he picked up.

"Hello, gorgeous. How are you?" Regardless of the story that had transpired between them, he still answered the phone like they were together.

"Corey, I need help. I'm not okay." Amelia's raspy voice slurred through her story of the pills, of drinking wine, of sobbing on the floor in defeat, of Luna crying.

"Where are they now?" Corey asked.

"I put them back in the bottle and away in the cabinet."

"Okay, have you thought about flushing them?"

"I did, but I haven't done it yet."

"Okay, that's fine. Why don't you do it now with me on the phone?"

Amelia wiped the dripping snot from underneath her nose with her shirt and stood up to collect the bottle. She pulled them out from the back of the medicine cabinet and unscrewed the lid. She stared at the bottle as she tipped it over the edge of the toilet watching them fall in slow motion.

Amelia flushed the toilet as every last pill cycled down the drain. "It's done."

"I'm really proud of you. Can I come over? I don't want you to be alone." Amelia melted onto the bathroom floor, unable to stand erect for a second longer.

"No, no you don't have to come over."

"I know I don't *have* to."

"I know, I know. You don't *have* to do anything. You want to. And I appreciate that. But honestly, you are the last person who would understand any of this. I just wanted to hear a voice. To know that someone would pick up on the other end. That if I died, laying on the bathroom floor, that it wouldn't be weeks or months before someone found me."

Corey the fixer. He couldn't just sit there on the other end of the line knowing Amelia was hurting, fearful for her life. And Amelia knew this, too. She continued to reassure him that she was going to be okay. That Luna stopped her in time, that she was the only one Amelia wanted to be with. Despite feeling so unbelievably lonely, she couldn't bear for anyone else to witness her in that state.

"I'll give you a call later this week. Thank you for answering the phone."

"Anytime. You know I'm just a phone call away. Always. Okay? Always."

"Thank you, Corey. Seriously."

"Just promise me you won't do anything you can't take back.

Promise?"

"I promise."

Amelia hung up the phone and stared off into the distance in a state of shock. She needed to be somewhere she felt safe. She dropped back onto all fours and crawled into bed. Luna didn't wait for her usual invite. She jumped up and buried her face in Amelia's armpit, pushing harder and harder until she flopped on top of Amelia's stomach.

Looking up at the ceiling, nearly swallowed by the deafening silence as she matted down Luna's soft fur, she wondered what was next. The shaking of her body and the spin cycle of her vision made it impossible to comprehend what had just happened, let alone what would come next.

But if she wasn't going to die, if this wasn't the end, what would the rest of her days look like? There had to be something, anything worth living for beyond the small scope of her world. Something that gave her purpose and drive every day. Something that made her remember why she was on this planet. She closed her eyes, clasped her hands together, rested her arm on Luna's back, and began to pray out loud. One final attempt to have God hear her eager prayers.

"God, I know I'm not the best Christian. I know that I don't go to church or pray or read the bible like I should. I know that I don't add any value to this world, and I know that I don't deserve anything from You. I really don't. But I'm at the end of my rope, and I just feel so lost. I don't know what to do, who to turn to, what to even ask for. Please God, just help me. Help me find a way out of this. I'm begging You. I'll do whatever it takes. Just please, help me. Make it stop, please. Amen."

Chapter 12

Amelia glanced at her phone to check the time. 7:31 a.m. It was the latest she'd slept in months. It was no surprise her body wanted to remain in a coma. She was still teetering on the edge of intoxication. The smell of alcohol seeped from her pores as she became cognizant of the hangover.

Last night. I can't believe...

She rubbed the palms of her hands heavily down her face, stretching her cheeks as if she could pull them right off. There were no words to describe the feeling of lying in bed with Luna curled up next to her, knowing she was still alive. God gave her a second chance for the hundredth time.

Her upper lip was raw from the constant drip of her nose. She didn't think it was possible to cry that much. Barely able to see through the foggy lenses of her eyes, Amelia rolled herself slowly off the bed and onto the floor. Luna popped her head up and cocked it to the side, confused at seeing Amelia as this old rag doll plummeting to the ground.

Although Amelia's inner monster yelled at her for not following through, she was able to exhale a sigh of relief at the fact that she had indeed failed at something as significant as this. It was a bittersweet feeling, and one she had no clue what to do with.

On the one hand, she'd stopped herself from ending her life. On the other, she was still in the exact same position as when the pills grazed her fingertips. There would have to be a change. She said this to herself every day, but after last night—when she'd seen the absolute deepest part of the world's oceans and managed to swim back to the top—she had to be able to do something about it today. There had to be a lesson behind this pain.

The only thing she knew for certain was that the moon and sun would come and go. A rotation that would continue even if Amelia wasn't around to greet them. Only on this day, she was.

It was Saturday and in just a few short hours, group therapy would start. She hadn't gone in weeks, not since she'd relapsed. How could she show her face to them when she was so ashamed? After months of talking about how well she was doing and how there was no way she could possibly fall off the wagon, she was back at square one. But Amelia was ready to face her peers and confront her truth.

In a daze, Amelia conjured up the last remaining ounces of her energy to prop herself up onto her feet. She turned on the shower ready to scrub away another layer of alcohol, cigarettes, and regret before she had to leave. She felt like she was somewhere in between Emmett's surviving and striving, an uncharted gray area she wasn't sure how to navigate.

Emmett. A dark cloud soared above her head. It was still too hard for her to think about him and their nascent friendship. She needed to stay focused. Even if she didn't take her turn to speak, she could still be in the presence of people who could come close to understanding her darkness. With one cigarette left, Amelia put Luna's harness around her chest and headed to the store.

She stepped through the front doors of her building. Everything looked new, like she was seeing it for the first time. The wind felt more intense brushing across her skin. The effervescent colors of the flowers stood out in ways she hadn't remembered since Machu Picchu.

The tops of her feet could feel the warmth from the sun through the webbing of her sandals. Life, on this day, was vibrant.

One block to the right onto 14th Street brought her the long way around—an attempt to avoid seeing Emmett on his usual morning smoke break. One more block on Pearl Street and they arrived at Capitol Convenience.

A young man in his early twenties worked there most days. Amelia had heard his name once but could never remember what it was. Instead, she called him Louisiana because he came from a place just outside of New Orleans and had a thick Southern accent. For some reason, she never felt ashamed or embarrassed walking into the convenience store as a complete train wreck. He always had a smile and a sincere, welcoming demeanor that made Amelia feel more invited than anywhere else she'd been since moving into the neighborhood.

Amelia tied up Luna's leash to the street pole like she did every other time she went there. Luna was visible through the windowed storefront. That way she could keep an eye out in case anything ever happened. She was only ever inside a minute or two. Amelia kissed the top of Luna's head and went inside. Louisiana was working the register, smiling per usual.

"Good mornin'! How's your day goin' so far?"

Amelia's hair was wet and disheveled, the soaking snarls barely covered by the hood of her gray sweatshirt. Her pink hexagon sunglasses hid most of her face, including her sunken cheeks and the purple bags under her eyes.

"Off to a bangin' start, if you couldn't tell," Amelia responded with sarcastic finger guns, a vain attempt to keep him at a distance.

"Oof, I've definitely been there before."

Louisiana continued to spew out words Amelia couldn't snatch from the air between them. Normally she loved listening to his delightful Southern accent, but she was so hungover she couldn't get herself to focus. All she wanted was to smoke a cigarette and have her coffee.

As she faked a smile to pretend she was paying attention, she heard a desperate wail from outside of the convenience store. Amelia looked out the window and saw Luna on the ground, twitching on her back and yelping at the top of her lungs.

"Oh my God!" Amelia dropped everything, leaving her debit card and newly purchased cigarettes on the counter, and ran to Luna. She fell to the ground, hitting the concrete with her knees. She picked up Luna's head and rested it on her lap to caress her face. There was a smear of blood underneath her back right leg in the shape of a dog bite, but thankfully nothing that wouldn't heal on its own. Amelia shook with a mixture of rage and fear.

"Who the hell did this!?" Amelia screamed out loud, looking around to find the culprit. She spotted a tall, lanky man with his dog's leash in one hand and a skateboard in the other. It was Kyle, one of the people who lived in her building. He was always high on something and had an energy that made Amelia steer clear of him.

His black, German Shepherd mutt sat patiently by his feet, acting as if nothing had happened.

"I'm so sorry," Kyle said with remorse barely skimming past his lips. "He's usually really friendly."

"I don't care! Just get your dog out of here!"

"Do you need help? Do you want me to pull my car around? There's an animal hospital just a few blocks up. I can take you."

Amelia ignored him. All she could focus on was Luna. Amelia didn't even know it was possible for a dog to cry, but the droplets drenched the fur on Luna's face nonetheless.

Luna curled herself tighter into Amelia's lap. She lightly held Luna's mouth shut to get her to stop howling. She petted her face and cooed at Luna to calm her down.

"It's okay, shhh, you're okay," Amelia reassured her, even though she knew Luna wouldn't understand what she was saying. After another minute of laying on the sidewalk together, Luna finally slowed her breathing and fell silent, resting in her mother's lap.

"Here's your card and smokes, everythin' alright?" Louisiana came up behind her to see if he could help without getting in trouble for leaving the store. Amelia exhaled deeply, realizing that in an attempt to calm Luna down, she'd forgotten to breathe herself. She extended her hand to accept her items she'd left behind that he'd graciously brought out to her.

"Ya, she's okay. I think she was just scared because that stupid dog bit her. Thank you though I really appreciate it."

"Wait one second." Louisiana ran back inside and within a few seconds, jogged back over to hand Amelia a tissue. Holding Luna in her arms like a baby on the dirty cement, Amelia didn't notice she'd been crying.

In theory, the idea of something bad happening to Luna seemed impossible. But Amelia never understood the detriment it would cause—not if, but when—something bad actually happened to her. She wanted to protect her child and would do whatever it took to make sure that she was okay. That she was safe. That she was alive.

After a few more minutes on the ground, Amelia tried to encourage Luna to stand up.

"Slowly," she said out loud to Luna in the same way she prompted herself through her own vertigo. Luna hobbled for a few steps and immediately found her puppy-pep again. How simple.

If Luna can do it, why can't I?

They walked back to their building, up the three flights of stairs, and into their apartment. Amelia took her shirt off and used it to dab the blood off of Luna's leg. The dog winced every so often, pushing deeper into Amelia's side for comfort.

I wonder if this is what Luna felt last night. She almost lost me, and I almost lost her. What would I have done?

All this time, Amelia had been searching for purpose, for someone who needed her. And all the while, Luna was by her side every single day. Connection. Like everyone else she ignored and pushed away. Other people she'd let go of and excommunicated from her life. Amelia wasn't alone, she chose to be lonely.

Time was going by fast and Amelia needed to shake off the jitters from the morning's fiasco. She didn't want to leave Luna alone, especially after what just happened. But if Amelia was going to find a way towards a healthy recovery so she could take care of Luna and be there for the long run, she had to take care of herself first. Amelia needed human connection. She needed her group. Her ED—eating disorder—family.

When it was finally time to leave, she smothered Luna with kisses, trying to instill certainty in Luna that she'd soon return. Ten minutes later, she pulled up to a parking spot a few hundred feet away from the front doors of the Eating Disorder Foundation (EDF). They were a nonprofit in Denver that provided support groups, mentors, and other resources for those with eating disorders and their loved ones. It was an old house that was renovated with a few office spaces, but still maintained a homey feeling.

Amelia sat in the driver's seat, trying to find an ounce of willpower to get her out of the car and through the front door. It reminded her of the first time she went to group therapy sitting outside those same doors.

She remembered being buried inside an oversized, neon yellow sweatshirt and her usual gray sweatpants with her hair clipped back in an unkempt bun. Dominic had dropped her off because she knew that if she went on her own, she'd never be able to get herself inside. Amelia spent the next hour and a half sitting quietly in the corner of the room with her legs pulled up to her chest and tears pouring down her cheeks while she listened to men and women talk about their experiences. She didn't share, she only listened.

This is not your first group session. You've done this before and you can do it again. You've got this.

Amelia finished her pep talk, turned off the car and walked towards the house. A bell chimed above her as she opened the door. A jovial woman sat at the front desk.

"Hey! I'm so glad you're here!" Amelia let out a slight grin, thinking about Miranda and her very similar comforting welcome. The woman's name was Naomi and she had been there for Amelia's very first introduction to EDF. She helped her sign the confidentiality paperwork and sat with her so Amelia could express any fears or anxieties she had about being there. Naomi was warm, with long, blond hair and adorable, brown, square-framed glasses that sat perfectly on her face.

Amelia still had a few minutes before the group started so she went into the kitchen to make herself a cup of coffee. The kitchen on the downstairs level always had mixed nuts, pretzels, peanut M&Ms, and granola bars. The pantry was always stocked with coffee and creamer and was open for anyone if they needed a safe space to eat without fear of judgement. The foundation was more of a community than it was a support group. It was another home for Amelia, even if it was one she was still hesitant to accept.

Amelia grabbed her cup of coffee and headed up the stairs. Inside the support group meeting room was a table, about ten chairs, and five giant bookshelves that were filled with self-help books, literature, and art supplies for the Thursday art therapy group. Amelia tried it a few times, but drawing was never really her medium for expression.

During one of the art sessions, she drew an eyeball crying, creating a wave that grew from the roots of a tree with the sun shining above. When the group shared their responses to her sketch, Amelia's picture received so much more love than she'd expected. Each person was able to take away something different from it. Amelia framed her picture as a reminder that, no matter how terrible a situation may seem, everything boils down to perspective.

There were about eight people who regularly attended the group, all of whom were individuals who provided her with new and different outlooks on living with eating disorders. They ranged from twenty-eight to sixty-nine and came from different walks of life.

One person had Dissociative Identity Disorder (once called multiple personality disorder), another attendee was on her last few rounds of chemo. There was a young homeless man with his service dog who lost everything he had from his disorder after hiding his sexuality from his family for years. Some attendees were retired teachers, some were unemployed, and some were successful business leaders. Regardless of where they came from, they all had one thing in common: food ruled their life.

She'd forgotten what it was like to be surrounded by such diverse people with different stories, all trying to negotiate with the same inner monsters as she. An empty lounge chair sat in the back corner of the room, the exact same chair from her first visit to EDF, inviting her to have a seat. She waved hello to her fellow group members, took off her shoes, and made herself comfortable.

The moderator walked into the room and sat down at the head of the table with a bright, white smile slapped across her face. Her brunette pixie cut and relaxed demeanor eased any last traces of Amelia's discomfort.

"Hey everyone, I'm so glad you all are here today," she said to the room. Just like Naomi and Miranda. "I see some new faces, so for those of you that don't know me, my name is Carmen. I'm a psychiatrist here in Denver and have been running this group on Saturdays for a few weeks now." Her voice was soothing, providing comfort to each person in the room.

Every group session started with the guidelines. Each person would read one of the bulleted rules and pass the list onto the next attendee who was comfortable reading out loud. Once all the rules were read, the checklist was handed back to Carmen so she could facilitate the meeting.

"I don't know how everyone has done this before," Carmen said, settling back in her chair and taking off her own shoes, "but I personally prefer the 'popcorn' style. If you are ready and want to speak, feel free to chime in. Share your name, your pronouns, and your highs and lows for the week. Whatever you need to talk about, this is a safe space and we're all here to support one another."

The room fell silent. Per usual. No one ever wanted to be the first person to speak, regardless of how many times they attended. Finally, an older gentleman started talking.

"I guess I'll go first. My name is Rob. He, him, his. I'm sixty-nine-ye ars-young, or at least I like to think. My wife on the other hand, not so much. I'm just going to start by saying this week has been a rough one."

Rob didn't fit the stereotypical image of a person with an eating disorder, i.e., a white female in her twenties seeking validity in a diet-cultured world of social media acceptance. Rob was, in some regards, the opposite. He'd lived with his experience for decades of under-eating and overexercising, believing that his only means of self-worth came from being "manly," just like his parents expected him to be. It wasn't until his son was born that his life changed, and then even more so when he had to get knee surgery making him completely immobile.

Amelia knew Rob as well as you can know someone from a weekly hour and a half meeting. He always brought a laugh into the room, even when the ambiance otherwise screamed turmoil and awkwardness.

Rob was honest and vulnerable when he spoke. After years of dealing with his eating disorders, he knew that he needed inpatient treatment. However, being a man in his fifties in an eating disorder recovery center made him the odd ball out. There were a few other males there, but no one of his age. According to Rob, he wouldn't have had it any other way.

"I hear these stories you all share here, especially the young women, and my heart aches. I just want to protect you from all of the hurt and pain that you've gone through, that you're going through now, and know that I can't.

"But that experience has also made me see how much work I need to do as a man in our society. I carry so much guilt for the way I've treated people, especially women, throughout my life. I need to stop being a part of the problem and start to be a part of the solution. It's shameful, but I have to own it."

Rob's genuine desire to make amends for his past was clear—his poor behavior as a father, husband, and a human of his generation. They were catalysts for his eating disorder and knew he had to address these issues if he wanted to sustain his recovery. Amelia understood that. There were layers beneath her surface she was still pulling back, trying to see why she had this disorder in the first place. The lesson behind the pain.

A few more people, including Amelia, shared about their weeks. Some were optimistic over new jobs, achieving their weekly meal plans, or getting out of treatment. Others were more solemn, struggling to understand why they couldn't manage to have a functioning relationship or were falling back into disordered behaviors after years of managing them. Each story was unique, yet all were too familiar.

An hour and a half later, the group ended and people began to file out the door. A woman about Amelia's age came up behind her.

"Hey, Amelia."

She turned around to see a beautiful girl with a head of voluminous, brown curls, bobbed right at the shoulders, approaching her. "My name is Jen, but you probably already knew that." Amelia didn't. She was terrible with names. "I wanted to say that what you share in the group resonates a lot with me. I also have bipolar disorder and when you mentioned that a few months ago I wanted to make you something. I just haven't seen you around to be able to give it to you."

Jen handed Amelia a piece of black construction paper, maybe a little larger than a postcard. On one side she'd pasted a photograph of a colorful porcelain toilet, jauntily placed in an overgrown garden of weeds and wildflowers. On the reverse was a note written with a white glitter gel pen.

"You don't have to read it now, but I put my phone number on there in case you ever want to grab a coffee and talk sometime. I feel like we have a lot in common and wanted to let you know how grateful I am that you come here, even if we haven't had a chance to get to know each other. But I really hope that changes."

Amelia was stunned. A complete stranger had done something thoughtful for her, just like Emmett with his cardboard Horror. But Jen wasn't really a stranger. At the end of the day, these people in her group knew her better and more authentically than most people she'd known her entire life. They knew her inner demons. They understood the feelings she had in her darkest hours because they'd all been there once, twice, or fifty times before. Her eyes welled up with tears.

"Can I hug you?" Amelia always asked permission. Hugging could turn some people to dust.

Jen didn't hesitate to open her arms and embrace Amelia with her frail, beautiful, recovering body. Amelia folded herself tightly into Jen. She'd never hugged someone else with an eating disorder before. She wondered if this is what other people felt when they hugged her. It felt so good. All she could do was cry and ignore the fact that she'd been probably holding onto the hug for a little longer than was socially acceptable.

They exchanged their goodbyes and Amelia walked out of the room. Rob was slowly making his way down the stairs, holding onto the railing for support.

"Hey Rob, mind if I help?"

He smiled at Amelia in a fatherly way and extended his left arm for Amelia to loop hers through. They took their time, going down each step with precision, until they made it outside and onto the sidewalk. Rob stopped abruptly.

"Is everything okay?" Amelia asked, concerned his knee might be bothering him.

"No, everything is fine. I just want to say I'm so glad you come to these groups." His hands were shaking, not from nerves, but because his aging body barely had control anymore. "Ever since I first heard you speak, you've changed so much for me. Your words are so inspiring. I'm so glad I met you and am privileged to have you in my life. Thank you for sharing what you do."

A smile grew across Amelia's face. This had to be a sign from God. Both Jen and Rob were like lanterns that had finally been refilled and relit, guiding Amelia through the dark. She asked for permission to hug Rob and with open arms he accepted.

It was unbelievable how much could change if she simply allowed people in. In just a few short hours, her entire perspective had shifted. There was a warmth inside of her she hadn't felt in so long: *she* was needed by others. *They* needed *her*, not the other way round.

Luna needed her alive. Her extended family found significance in Amelia's words. More importantly, Amelia's definition of purpose—her reason to exist for which she'd been searching—was in front of her face the entire time. She'd been too caught up in running away from her inner demons to see it. Amelia knew what she needed to do next.

She needed to talk to Emmett.

Chapter 13

The faint sound of the radio played in the background as Amelia gripped the steering wheel with both hands. The love she'd received from her group refueled her and she wasn't ready to give that feeling up just yet. She rolled down all four windows, plugged her phone into the auxiliary jack, and hit play on the song "You Can Call Me Al" by Paul Simon. It was her life anthem, the one song she'd always turn to when everything else seemed in disarray.

She sang the words at the top of her lungs, making up the ones she didn't know despite how many years she'd been listening to the song on repeat. It lifted her higher and higher as the trumpets progressed.

Amelia stuck her arm out of the window and felt the wind twine through her fingers. The simple act of driving could change her entire attitude. It was a tool she'd forgotten about and was finally dusting off.

A few minutes later, she turned onto 14th Street and pulled into her garage. She turned off the ignition and sat with her keys in her hands.

Amelia had a choice. She could walk upstairs to wallow and let the debilitation kick in, or she could make one small decision to keep moving forward.

Talking to Emmett was the next right move for her. Despite their argument, she didn't want to leave their friendship on bad terms and have their fight be the last time they spoke. She wanted to clear the air, even if it still resulted in the two of them going their separate ways.

She wondered if his Amelia senses were tingling and if he would reach out to her. But that was her entire life, never taking action and always hoping for something to happen. She picked up her phone and made the next move. One text was all she needed to see if he wanted anything to do with her or not.

AMELIA: Hey, are you busy?

She waited patiently for her phone to vibrate with his response, but there was nothing. She couldn't be disappointed because that would have meant she had expectations, and she reminded herself that there was no need for that kind of pressure.

Amelia finally got out of the car and went upstairs to be reunited with Luna. She opened the front door to find Tuna Bean directly in front of the entrance and wiggling her entire body. She barked a song of love. Amelia dropped to the floor and grabbed a hold of the puppy's relentless body. Luna leaped up and wrapped her paws around Amelia's neck like a human. It was hard to see the extraordinary and simplistic joys in life when the cloud of depression obstructed the view. Amelia's cloud was dissipating, and her vision was clearing.

Amelia's phone vibrated in her back pocket. It was Emmett.

EMMETT: Sorry, I was napping.

Of course he was. In her very short time knowing him, she'd learned he was a big proponent of frequent, twenty-minute cat naps. Amelia texted back so she wouldn't lose his attention.

AMELIA: I know things have been weird, but would you like to talk?

EMMETT: Ya, that would be nice.

Amelia decided it was best to leave Luna at home so she could give her undivided attention to Emmett. Even though Luna provided her emotional support, this was a battle Amelia needed to fight on her own. She walked downstairs and saw him waiting on the stoop lighting a cigarette. Amelia hesitantly walked towards the stairs and sat down on a step below him, keeping a few feet of distance between them. They skipped their usual warm embrace.

"I went to my group therapy today." Amelia wasn't going to waste any time basking in awkward silence.

"I wish they had a group for people like me, but that might be a fire hazard." Even though they were fighting, Emmett still managed to come through with a joke.

"Ya, I thought about you a lot actually." The silence lingered; clearly Emmett didn't know what to say, which seemed unusual for him, even in uncomfortable circumstances. "Are you okay with"—Amelia pointed her index finger back and forth between her and Emmett—"well, with *this?*"

"No. I mean yes, it's fine. It's not like I have a lot going on right now, anyways. I've just been sketching ideas for a character in the book I'm working on." Emmett showed her a drawing of a monster wearing high heels and a torso made of a clawfoot bathtub.

"And you can draw, too? What can't you do?"

"Can we *not* pretend to have a normal conversation?" Emmett was right. Amelia needed to muster the courage to face her fears.

"Fair enough." Amelia rubbed both of her ear lobes, took a deep breath, and looked directly into Emmett's eyes despite how uncomfortable it made her. "I couldn't stop thinking about what you told me. About dancing with your demons and survival days and all of the amazing things you've shared with me and have let me share with you. I know that you feel a certain way about me, and when I'm ready to date again, I will. But I don't want to lead you on to think that you and

I will be together."

It was empowering to stand up for herself, for her wants and her needs, even if it meant that she had to hurt someone else's feelings in the process. Emmett had a discouraged disposition about him, but he shrugged his shoulders in his cartoon-esque way and said the words Amelia needed to hear.

"I can handle you being with someone else. What I can't handle is the silence."

Amelia was relieved. With one sentence Emmett was able to explain that he'd rather Amelia be upfront with him instead of her usual cold silence of submission.

"Question for you: When you made it out, when you finally felt like you had control over your mental illness, did you know it? Or did it just happen?" Amelia looked down at her feet as she posed the question.

Emmett rolled another cigarette between his tar-stained fingers. His nails were bitten down to nubs.

"There wasn't an exact moment, partly because I'm not out of the woods. I feel like I have a handle on it now, more so than I have in the past. But it doesn't mean that I don't have hard days. The demons still come out, my walls still turn into worms occasionally, and I find myself to be sad more often than not." He took a drag of his cigarette.

"But what I do know is that I'm finally at a place of independence. I don't rely on my disease to carry me through life because it's familiar or comfortable. I can be on my own and be content with that because I love who I am."

"I just don't know if I can do that, not on my own."

"Amelia, things are never going to be easy. You know that, right? You know that this is something you'll live with for the rest of your life. You'll go in and out of various coping mechanisms and you'll find yourself at the bottom of the barrel a dozen times more. But that doesn't mean you can't always get yourself out of that barrel. Because you'll have done it eleven times before that, and each time you'll be stronger than the last.

"It's like making art. You're the only authority when it comes to creating something. But release it into the world and every person who comes across it is going to misunderstand or reinterpret it. But it's a beautiful mess of a creation that only *you* could have created. Just like your disorders, just like you. You wouldn't throw these things away because they've made you who you are. It's a matter of what you do with them and what you allow them to mean to you."

As always, Emmett knew the right thing to say, even when they weren't on good terms. And he was right, which made her slightly sad and afraid.

"Can I be honest about something?" Amelia was on a roll and wanted to be true, down to her core, about what she was thinking and feeling, even if it wasn't what he wanted to hear. She had to put herself first.

"If you haven't learned by now, I wouldn't want it any other way," Emmett responded.

"As much as I would love for us to mend whatever transpired this week, I don't know if I can keep this friendship. At least not right now."

"Can I ask why?"

Amelia searched for another cigarette to give her something to do with her hands. "Because...because you're right. I need to do this for myself, only I can save myself. I think I've been using you as a crutch, which pains me to say because I'm hurting you and acknowledging a hugely shitty piece of myself. Even before I met you, I told myself that you were my guardian angel who always had my back when I wasn't looking."

A hot flash swam through Amelia's body. The remaining traces of alcohol oozed from her clammy skin. She refused to stop the flow of honesty. She just hoped Emmett couldn't smell the alcohol that was burning through her clothes.

Amelia continued before she lost her courage, "I was drawn to you for whatever reason. To your energy, to some kind of great, divine, imaginary intervention. Regardless, I clung to you. And once you became tangible, I didn't want to let you go. You reminded me what it's like to laugh—like *genuinely* laugh. You reminded me that there are still amazing humans on this planet. But you also reminded me of the work I still need to do. Work that I need to do alone."

There was another bout of silence.

"I guess you could say that you are a vice I need to stop abusing as a coping mechanism."

She waited patiently for him to say something to reaffirm that what she said wasn't a total mistake.

"Well,"—Emmett blew smoke up towards the sky—"you should know, there are significant withdrawal symptoms for the first two weeks, but I'm sure you'll manage."

She couldn't tell if he was joking or not, but as a smile began to spread beneath his rectangular black frames, she knew; he understood.

"I've been there, Amelia, and I get it. You might not think that's true, but I do. Doesn't mean it doesn't hurt a little, though." Emmett stood up from his throne. "I think I'm gonna get going. I need to decompress from everything."

"Sounds like a great plan," Amelia responded in an empathetic tone.

"I just want you to know one thing before we part ways. I want you to be happy. That's all. Let yourself do what you need to do to get out of this damn hole. Go find yourself someone who will treat you the way you deserve. Life isn't meant to be experienced alone."

Amelia smiled and started to walk away.

"One last thing: To aspire is to strive towards a goal. To aspirate is to breathe. Breathing is just striving towards life." Emmett never was short for words.

Breathing is just striving towards life.

She thought about what song would play in the background of her life at that moment. Something fun that would make her want to dance, something that would make her feel free. She walked through her apartment door and crouched down to pet Luna, who wiggled with enthusiasm after having been left alone a total of twenty minutes. Amelia could tell she was feeling much better after her own confrontation with an unfriendly beast of a dog.

She walked over to her record player and put on "Jump In The Line" by Harry Belafonte, another one of her favorites.

Striving towards life...

She swayed back and forth to the rhythm so as to not overdo it. For once she was listening to what her body needed, which was not to be thrown around in elaborate dance moves. She closed her eyes and pretended to see them, this perfect stranger who would one day complement her life, not over fill it. She pretended to embrace this figment of a person.

Maybe it was possible this human existed somewhere in the universe. She carefully danced around the living room with her imaginary partner. This person wouldn't change her or add something that was missing because Amelia wasn't incomplete and there wasn't anything to add. Alone, she'd be strong like a fort. Together they'd be an army, protected and safe from all of the world's problems. They'd encourage her to write or listen to her favorite music again, to laugh until she cried or cried until she laughed, to do whatever made her heart content. As long as she was happy, they'd support her.

Amelia continued down into her daydream, only this time it was a memory yet to come.

They lived in a brick house, tucked away in a remote corner of the world. Vines cascaded down the bamboo fence and sounds of water trickling from a nearby fountain filled the air. Birds chirped and a group of squirrels created their home in the backyard. A hawk made a guest appearance followed by the sound of people passing by on their morning commutes. Tiny little paws burrowed their way into the dirt, creating a comfortable nook for Luna's white, furry stomach.

Humidity lightly coated the air, just enough to remind her that, even on the driest of days, rain would come to replenish the Earth. Her mystery person walked over and hugged her. There was something about their energy that radiated a type of love that kept Amelia calm.

"I've got your back." This person who spoke to her was a stranger, but Amelia felt like she knew them for years. "When you're ready, I'm here. I love you."

Before she had a chance to catch her breath, she awoke from her trance. Back to a reality where she was alone, only this time she was relieved. This fictitious person she'd conjured in her subconscious was the person Emmett alluded to. This was the person she knew she'd one day be with. But for now, she was perfectly content with the solitude.

Her only desire at that moment was to be the red velvet cake.

She'd given away a slice of her cake to every person who entered her life. But the last slice, that last sliver of sweetness that was left on the plate, was hers. The best part was, if she ever ran out, she had the recipe in her possession. She could make the cake over and over again, always refilling her fork with the next delectable bite until she was ready—just like in her daydream—until she found someone *worthy* to share it with. Until someone came into her life who found joy in the cake without any modifications.

Amelia started to believe there could be a future for herself. And the future tasted delicious.

Luna walked over to the front door and started to whine. With her energy levels back up, Amelia thought she should try and get Luna to walk out any last bit of pain that might be left in her bitten leg. The 16th Street Mall was one place she hadn't explored yet since moving in. The sun was brutal, but the two girls needed to feel the embrace of its rays.

Of course, as soon as they reached the near end of the mall, about a ten-minute walk from the apartment, Amelia saw a raindrop fall onto the sidewalk. Then another. Then on her face. That was Amelia's cue to turn around and try to avoid the oncoming and unexpected rain. Within seconds, hail the size of marbles began to fall from the sky, the pellets bouncing off of her skin. Amelia tugged at Luna's leash to get her to start running. Amelia had on sandals that were worn too thin, not the optimal shoes for running down the busy sidewalks of Denver. Everyone around her was looking for cover. Amelia kept running and Luna frantically jumped around trying to eat the hail that was coming down.

About two minutes in, Amelia stopped. The soles of her feet were hurting and the running somehow seemed to make the hail feel worse. She was already soaking wet. She slowed down her pace and admitted defeat. The boy in the yellow swim shorts. A child who would never know the significant role he played in Amelia's story.

This is my life.

She burst into laughter. For the first time, completely on her own and without the aid of intoxication to lubricate her mind, Amelia found laughter. Amelia found joy. Amelia was happy.

Chapter 14

Sunday, a day of rest.

Growing up, her parents would rally the troops for church every Sunday morning. This was followed by a trip to Dunkin' Donuts for a dozen delicious treats as a reward if everyone sang their songs and were well behaved throughout mass. Another long-forgotten ritual.

A subtle hint of sunlight glowed through the bedroom window, gently waking her from a dream she couldn't remember, but recalled being something wonderful. It was one of those dreams where she'd wake up with a smile stamped across her face for no other reason than a fictional story created in her subconscious that she already couldn't recollect.

Amelia rolled over on her side to snuggle Luna, as per usual, but she wasn't there. Amelia sat up and saw Luna waiting by her bedside, ready to conquer the day. No snuggles necessary.

She got up and performed her morning routine. Rinse. Wash. Repeat. Another Sunday, another day, another week ready to pass her by. As she was brushing her teeth, she looked down to see Luna playfully rolling around on her back.

But it doesn't have to be just another Sunday, another day, or another week.

If Luna had taken the opportunity to change one tiny thing about her day by sitting at the foot of the bed, Amelia wanted to see if she could do the same. To rewrite the narrative, as Miranda would say. Amelia decided to make one small change in her routine. She pulled open her dresser drawer and grabbed a pair of running shorts, a sports bra, a T-shirt, and socks. She slipped into every item like they were long-lost friends she hadn't seen in a while.

There was a period of time when exercise transformed from being an extracurricular activity into orthorexia, a disorder that created her unhealthy relationship with exercise. She couldn't just go for a casual jog or spend an hour at the gym. The more calories she consumed, the more she'd exercise to counterbalance what she ate, to burn more than devoured. It had been months since she last exercised, aside from her usual walks with Luna throughout the day. It was time for Amelia to go back to the thing she loved once upon a time.

Running was how Amelia managed to cope with her anxiety before the panic became an unmanageable problem. Her anxiety and depression only worsened when her doctor told her she needed to take a break from running and most other forms of exercise. The lack of control over what she could and couldn't do with her body only exacerbated her anxiety. But she obeyed the doctor's orders.

Amelia proceeded to look around her apartment. A random assortment of papers, notebooks, bags, and dirty clothes were scattered throughout. Piece by piece she picked everything up and put each item in its proper place.

Amelia hadn't made her usual morning cup of coffee. She hadn't gone for her cigarette on the balcony. She hadn't sat down to try writing. Something was pushing at her from the inside of her soul, like a kinetic energy sending her forward.

I want to survive this. I want to have a future. I want to live.

She stood in the middle of the barren room, staring at the balcony doors. There was still time for her to change her mind about whether or not she'd go outside to smoke. Amelia unlocked the latch of the door and stepped outside. She grabbed the ashtray on the patio table and dumped the remains of her cigarette butts into the garbage. With only two cigarettes left in her pack, she made a bold move and threw them away to be buried with the ashes.

What next?

Luna whined at her feet. Maybe this was why Luna had switched things up for them. Maybe this was God's way of reminding Amelia that things could be different.

She put on her Bluetooth headphones, grabbed her phone, and buckled Luna's harness. They ran downstairs and started jogging towards the Capitol building. Her chest was burning and her feet aching.

This is how you start. Somewhere. Anywhere. One foot in front of the other.

Amelia was barely able to keep up with Luna's pace. "Maybe, IDK" by Jon Bellion came through her headphones. This was another song that had changed her life. It was the one that solidified her desire to travel. The song had shifted the foreseeable future in a way she never expected.

The anxiety crept in, making it difficult for her to breathe. Her lungs were sending a signal through a thick layer of ash and smoke. Amelia picked up the pace, Luna beside her and ready for the race. She stuck out her chest and pushed through the anxiety, through the tears, through to the end.

They came around the corner of 13th Street and back through the gate of their apartment building. Barely able to bring her wobbly legs up the stairs, they finally made it home before they both crumbled to the entryway floor. Luna sprawled out on her stomach, panting through a giant smile on her face.

Once Amelia caught her breath, she went into the bathroom and turned on the shower. She washed her hair, shaved her legs, exfoliated her face, and removed the cloud of cigarette stench that smothered her. Another shower to scrub away everything that reminded her of the person she never wanted to become.

In a weird way, it felt like she was dominating Dominic, the person who got her to start smoking again and the person who couldn't kick the habit himself. But Amelia could. One small victory at a time.

She got out of the shower and dried herself off. Fresh clothes without the lingering smell of cigarettes. Amelia heard her phone vibrate on the nightstand. She looked down towards the screen and her smile was stripped away. She froze at the sight of Dominic's name, responding to Amelia's text she'd sent on her birthday almost four days ago.

She held her breath and opened the message.

DOMINIC: Hey. Yeah, I'm good. Got a little place near the beach in Mexico before I figure out what's next. Happy belated birthday, I didn't wanna fuck with your b-day by texting you. Hope everything is good with you and Luna, too.

Amelia contemplated the message, trying to decipher what name to give to the feeling she had. Another helpful tool provided by Miranda. Naming feelings helped her understand them, it gave Amelia the grace she needed to confront them.

Nothing. I feel absolutely nothing.

All this time she thought she was terrified to talk to Dom, to see his name pop up on her phone, or to hear the sound of his voice.

But when she saw his name, when she read the words, she felt nothing except a sudden urge to cry. They weren't tears over Dominic. On the contrary, she was so elated that the only way she could deal with how happy she felt was by crying. Amelia's fears were no longer there, gone like a leaf taken by the wind. She wasn't sure what this meant for her recovery, but what she did know was that she was free. What she would do with this newfound freedom was another thing all together.

If there was one take away from the last year and half living in Denver, it was that there was nowhere in the world she felt more at peace than in the mountains. It was cliché, but true. She knew exactly what she needed to do next. Amelia put on a pair of leggings and a tank top, not even considering that her arms would be exposed for everyone to see. She laced up her hiking boots, filled her CamelBak, and stuffed her day pack with headphones, dog treats, poop bags, and even a snack. She wanted to spend the rest of the day hiking in the woods with Luna.

Amelia was finding faith in herself. She wasn't about to let the momentum stop. A body in motion stays in motion. Newton's third law, only it was usually the other side of the law governing her life, a body at rest stays at rest. Not this time. Not this day. Her day of rest would have to wait. The mountains were calling, and Amelia was listening.

She'd have to drive at least an hour and half heading west to beat the heatwave the city was enduring. The hailstorm had passed after just a few minutes and with Colorado's unpredictable weather patterns, she was willing to take the chance it wouldn't happen again. She and Luna got in the car and started driving towards the highway, each turn taking her closer to their end destination. The farther she drove through the winding roads of rockslides, the less people would be around, and the greater the chance that she could find some solitude. Being alone was now a choice rather than an obligation dictated by her inner monster.

About an hour and forty-five minutes outside of Denver, Luna and Amelia arrived at Chicago Lakes Trailhead. The parking lot was almost full. With the beautiful weather on a Sunday morning, it was inevitable that people would be out for a day trip. She'd done this trail before, knowing it would usually be packed up until Idaho Springs Reservoir. If she made it beyond there, the trail was open for her. She got Luna out of the car, locked everything up, put on her headphones, and headed towards the trail.

Every step she took was more exhausting than the last. Her lungs couldn't keep up with the momentum of her body. Smoking had clearly done plenty of damage, but it was a reminder of what needed to be repaired.

"There'll be days like this, my mama said..." The voices of The Shirelles blasted through her headphones. How fitting. Her ankles weakened, but she continued to push through to the halfway point. The trail opened up to expose the miraculous scenery of Idaho Springs Reservoir. She found a secluded spot along the shore where there was a log she could tie Luna to, leaving enough slack to let her wander into the water.

Amelia could try to force herself to hike several more miles to the top of Chicago Lakes, or she could listen to her body and stay put. This was a prime moment for the voices to trickle in. Instead of beating herself up and allowing them to pursue her, she decided to rewrite the narrative.

Amelia sat on a rock facing the water. An exhausted, panting Luna to her left, a ring of mountains and tall, thin trees cradling them both. The clouds created a flawless proportion of sun and shade. Amelia's heart struggled to keep up even though she was sitting down. Her skin vibrated as she gasped for air. She inhaled as deep as she could, filling up her lungs to the brim, trying to slow her breathing. They'd burst if she inhaled any deeper. She counted to four and exhaled. Out with the old. Every second, every breath, every moment gone to be replenished with the new.

Luna, twisted in her leash, was covered in mud, dirt, and fallen brush. She smiled at Amelia with her mouth wide open and tongue bouncing to match her panting breath. Her own rhythm to her own song just like Mother Nature, this one a tune that only she and Amelia were able to hear.

The wind blew across Amelia's face as a fly gently landed on her arm. Its movements were quick and staggered. She looked back over at Luna—circling herself one, two, three times until she finally sprawled her long body, belly down, allowing herself a moment to rest with her mother.

A bird chirped from a tree above her, calling out for something, or maybe someone. A plane soared faintly overhead.

God was there in those mountains. He was the maker, the master, the painter, the sculptor. She could feel Him wrapping His arms around her, letting Amelia know that she wasn't alone, that she belonged—belonged to no one, to everyone, to nowhere, to everywhere. She belonged to Him and with Him. She was not alone, no matter how hard she'd tried to push Him away.

A moment of clarity engulfed Amelia, one that didn't tease her or trick her into believing it was only temporary. This could be her future: a life without worrying about the constant need to appease others, without letting others hold onto the reins of her life.

A bottle of pills could've ended everything...

And now here she was, sitting with God and a few strangers on a reservoir hidden in the mountains. Amelia was certain she could have the future she always wanted.

How she got here baffled her. All of the ups and downs and nights filled with drunken tears, sadness, and heartache. Alcohol had become her crutch towards self-destruction. She'd reached her breaking point two nights ago, the line she never wanted to cross. Amelia had to get clear about what that future was going to look like in order to ensure she never wound up at that dark place again.

A gray cloud slowly crept in. That was a common thing in the Rocky Mountains. A shift in the air pressure could bring on a storm within twenty minutes. Just like the hailstorm earlier. Once again, there was no way to ever predict Colorado weather.

Don't forget to look up.

Amelia laughed with herself as she thought about the old man in San Bernardino alle Ossa in Milan, Italy. A man who she hadn't thought of until just now when she shot her gaze towards the sky. She recalled the story he had told them in the famous church of bones.

The cold November air made the world around her feel somber. Thousands of Italian men and women filled the busy streets of Milan. It felt like being in New York City with big screen billboards lighting up the sea of skyscrapers. Musicians and street performers shared their crafts outside of the plaza, busking for tips. Men and women sold street food from along every corner of the hustling city.

Amelia was completely out of her element. The fast-paced city of models, fashion designers, and more tourists than she felt comfortable being around caused her to sink lower into herself. It ignited a strong desire to hide beneath more layers of sweaters and scarves, to cover every inch of her skin.

Dominic's need to keep moving had brought them to the hundredth church they'd visited since they began their travels three months prior. They walked the metropolis to Santuario di San Bernardino alle Ossa, a small chapel near the city center. It was no ordinary chapel. It was an ossuary, a resting place that held the skeletal remains of the dead.

Amelia and Dominic walked through the front doors and into an empty church. An altar stood directly in the center. Signs in Italian and English requested a small donation for entry. They dropped a few euros into the donation box and followed the velvet ropes that lead them into the room of bones.

Amelia looked around the chapel, her head taking in the walls that were decorated from floor to ceiling with hundreds—thousands—of human skulls. Bones filled the gaps in between. Ribs and femurs were stacked upon each other and tucked with precision behind wire mesh, forming the patterns and crosses that covered the entirety of the room. She was awestruck. The bones looked smaller than she had imagined. She'd thought the human skeleton was something much larger.

A tour group of teenagers walked into the chapel. They were led by an older gentleman with untamed gray hair who looked to be in his mid-sixties. Amelia heard the man speaking in English just outside of the front door. She couldn't help eavesdropping.

"Now, before we enter the chapel, I want you all to get in line. Close your eyes and put your hands on the shoulders of the person in front of you as I begin to tell you the tale behind the bones."

The man ushered a line of blind teenagers through the fifteen-foot-tall entryway.

"The official story is that in 1210, a nearby cemetery ran out of space to hold the remains of those who died and so they built this house of bones. But there is another story....."

The group circled up around him.

"Now, open your eyes."

The teenagers slowly opened their eyes, almost afraid to see their surroundings. One by one, their jaws dropped as they looked at the chamber of bones that encompassed them.

"Now, what do you notice about these skulls?" Amelia wanted to know what the man meant. She looked around but couldn't spot a difference, not that she regularly studied human skulls.

"Do they seem smaller to you?" Exactly what Amelia had just been pondering! The heads stared with their empty eye sockets.

"According to an old tale, these were the skulls and bones of children—orphans that had nowhere to be buried because they didn't have a family name to give them a proper burial place. So instead, they saved the remains here in this ossuary. Again, this is just one of many fables out there, but it is a possibility nonetheless."

He continued on with his tall tale, almost as if he were telling a ghost story to frighten the children. Amelia wasn't entirely convinced it was true, but the way he spoke was captivating.

Dominic walked into the pew and sat next to Amelia. They were silent, soaking up the indoor cemetery. After several minutes, the tour group began to file out one by one to wait while the others finished taking photos of the remains. As the last teenager left the building, the older gentleman came up next to Amelia and whispered something in her ear.

"Don't forget to look up." He pointed towards the ceiling and Amelia's head slowly followed. Just like the teenagers, her jaw dropped as if it were about to detach and fall from her face.

Above the darkened cemetery was one of the most beautiful murals she'd ever seen. With an almost three-dimensional affect, a massive painting lined the high-vaulted dome. Sun rays beamed through the clouds and cherubs playing harps flew across the mural. In all of the pain, suffering, and darkness there was beauty still overlooking the dead. Angels were watching from the sky, reminding mourned and mourner alike that there is more, there is light in the dark, there is hope. Death will level us all, but not always today. Amelia didn't want to waste another minute.

Amelia came back down to Earth as a drop of water hit her forehead directly between her eyebrows. She opened her eyes and saw that the gray clouds had become significantly denser. With the storm approaching fast, she packed up her belongings, untangled Luna, and proceeded back towards the three-mile trail of switchbacks and steep declines towards the car. As she started walking towards the trail, her brow furrowed. There was still one more thing left to do.

She returned to the water's edge. Amelia closed her eyes, inhaled deeply, and began to talk to Dominic, knowing he would never hear the words she was about to say out loud. But the words weren't meant for him. They were meant for Amelia.

"It's the first time I've been tucked away in the mountains alone since you left. Before it was always you and I. Dominic and Amelia. I think I was just afraid to do anything without you. You made me feel like I needed you, like my existence depended on yours. Everything with us felt like so much work and I am so damn tired of working for something that no longer exists.

"Once I got here, once I made the fifty-three-mile drive through the empty dirt roads winding through the mountain side with no one except Luna, I realized that I did this entire thing called 'life' once before—and not because of you, but because I loved it. I loved life once before you, and I can most certainly love it after you. I can do this alone, I can lead my life and be strong, innovative, smart, fearless, and brave. I can have a life filled with love, and I can have that without you. Goodbye, Dom. Thank you for leaving. Thank you for teaching me what it means to save myself."

She looked down at Luna.

"Ready?" Luna's excited paws pounced in place as she looked up at her mother. "Ya, me too, Luna." The two girls turned back around towards the trail and headed home. It was time for Amelia to plan for a future she never thought she'd have. The future she deserved.

Epilogue

"**M**editation with intention is one of the greatest things you can do for yourself." Miranda's words resonated in her head. "It's one thing to think about your future, but it's another to visualize it. Use all of your senses. Close your eyes and think about what you want your future to look like, smell like, taste like. What does the view expose when you remove the boulders and finally overcome your challenges?"

Amelia's mind wandered at a pace she could barely keep up with. The panic rose towards the surface of her skin, tickling with goosebumps up and down the length of her arms. Her thoughts were racing as if they held their foot on the gas, taking her from zero to a hundred in a matter of seconds. The future held more possibilities than ever.

Her future was on a ranch, a wall of mountains surrounding her while children and dogs played in raked up piles of autumn leaves. Amelia started looking up the cost of land further west and how much weight her compact SUV could tow so she could live out of a trailer.

Her future was working at a hostel in Cape Town. She typed "how to bring a dog to South Africa" into the search engine. Her future was in New York, in a city that constantly buzzed from millions of people running to and from their jobs, pursuing their dreams of becoming actors on Broadway or stockbrokers on Wall Street while she worked at a bar in Greenwich Village. Amelia shifted gears and started researching how much she needed to save in order to live in New York City. Her future was in Florida with her mom while they flipped houses together like the dynamic duo they were always meant to be. She scrolled through her phone to text someone who could teach her carpentry.

Amelia paced around the apartment along her usual path. Down the hall outside of her bedroom, through the dining room towards the doors of the balcony, and back up again. Her body shook with a constant humming that matched the ambiance filling the room.

I was doing so good. What happened? Why can't I slow down?

She wanted to run away. She wanted to make the thoughts in her head stop rushing into each other like a car crash you can't stop watching. The familiar thoughts of packing a bag and driving away were becoming too powerful. She was manic and could see herself falling right back into the vicious cycle, the hamster wheel of chaos.

Amelia leaned her back against the wall in the hallway and slid down to the floor. She pulled her legs towards her chest and laid her forehead across the tops of her knees.

Breathe. Just breathe. You have the tools.

The tools. With her eyes closed, she inhaled on a four count, held her breath on a four count, and exhaled on a four count.

You can either dwell on and endure the tired, or you can find the message, your call to action to do something about it. Soul farts, Amelia.

She pulled the neck of her shirt above her eyes and held it shut to block out any light. She continued to breathe deeply and tried to slow down her thoughts.

I can do this, but I have to slow down.

She had to acknowledge that there was still a lot of dark she could very easily fall back into. Amelia was the one that held the power, not her inner monster. With the lights of her own universe shut off, she continued to breathe and painted a mental picture of her future.

She sat at a coffee shop, writing, while someone played the piano in the background. She had a cup of coffee, a notebook, and Luna laying by her feet. Her neighbors surrounded her; a community of individuals who lived the slow life. Never rushing, just existing with contentment. She wrote stories about the people she saw, about the tiny licks Luna gave her toes through the tops of her sandals. Her arms were exposed and she didn't even worry that someone might notice her triceps sagging just a bit from age.

She was transported to the backyard of a small bungalow where her children played. She could keep up with them because she quit smoking. Her hair was long with hints of gray, which her future partner adored; a man whose face she couldn't quite see. There were lights strung throughout the yard. Friends both new and old gathered together for a celebration: the release of Amelia's book.

Amelia's eyes shot open as she tilted her chin towards the empty room.

She knew what she wanted her life to look like. She was just taking the long way round.

As a child, she'd written elaborate stories about being a photographer, a flight attendant, or a middle school teacher. She made up overly fantasized tales about her family vacations and holiday gatherings. Amelia had spent her life writing down scenarios she'd conjured in her head, always wishing they were her reality.

Amelia ran to the hallway closet and grabbed a giant whiteboard and dry erase markers. She pulled out a chair from the dining room table and propped the whiteboard against the chair back. She knelt down on the floor, directly in front of the blank board. Purple marker in hand, she began to scribble out the thoughts racing through her mind.

She scrawled out different story ideas, subplots, and feelings she wanted to explore. She wrote down situations and people she'd come across throughout her life. She set the scene with words that made her feel the grass beneath her feet.

She looked outside towards the balcony. Thick clouds were coming through, alluding to a storm that would last the rest of the evening. Amelia knew, just like Monday, that it would feel like morning all night long. It was the perfect setting in which to write. She had nowhere to go, and everywhere to explore.

After an hour of purging her thoughts onto the whiteboard, she pulled back and saw a beautiful, breathtaking mural of organized chaos that would change her life forever. She saw what she'd been searching for, her future smeared across white plastic in purple marker. She felt like the writer she wanted to be, the writer she always was.

A slight twinge of doubt shot into her stomach.

Would anyone ever actually read what I have to say? How could I possibly do this? This is irrational. I'm just being manic. I'm getting too far ahead of myself and shouldn't be so over the top.

She closed her eyes and took four more deep breaths. This wasn't irrational. This wasn't a manic, impulsive moment. Her body was telling her that this was her truth. And her body never lied.

Amelia could feel the withdrawals from not having a cigarette; she wasn't ready to cave. A sharp pain abruptly pierced her fingers. She looked down at her hands and saw that she'd clasped them together tight enough that her rings had cut into her skin. As she opened her palms up towards the ceiling, tears followed suit.

It was as if she was seeing them for the first time. She'd written down her darkest thoughts in eclectic, yet poetic ways with these same hands for years, but, somehow, they still felt like strangers. Each and every line that contoured her hands seemed brand new to her in a matter of seconds. The way the skin broke along her knuckles. The brittle flakes of skin stung with every flex. They didn't look like the hands of a thirty-year-old. These hands had seen pain, extreme temperatures, and an obvious lack of care. These hands were tired.

Amelia finally gained the courage to lift her head up from her aging claws. Her fingers slowly caressed the edges of her pants, feeling the cotton matted with sweat from anxiety. Silence filled the room, vibrating with anticipation.

Now get up, Amelia.

She quickly stood up from her chair. A blanket of white covered her vision. Small, spotted stars floated around making everything feel slightly off kilter. She put all of her weight onto her hand against the back of the chair to keep her standing.

I have to eat. I can't do anything about creating a damn future for myself if I'm not alive to witness it. I have to eat.

She opened the junk drawer in the kitchen and sifted through an assortment of takeout menus from Chinese restaurants, breakfast diners, and food trucks throughout Denver. She finally landed on a locally owned sandwich shop around the corner from her apartment. Amelia picked up her phone and called the number on the menu, ordering herself a portobello mushroom sandwich with goat cheese on a hoagie roll. The person on the other line said it would be ready in fifteen minutes. In that moment, Amelia had taken a piece of Miranda's advice and dialed in on her emergency list. One small victory.

Amelia went into her bathroom to splash water on her face. She grabbed a towel, dried her cheeks, and opened her eyes. She shifted her gaze upwards towards the mirror. She had to test herself, to see if she truly had what it took for that next step. Amelia began examining her face in her reflection.

The bags under her eyes were exaggerated by her puffy eyelids. She stretched the skin on her face, starting from the corners of her lips and moving up along the curvature of her jaw line. She held it tight just below her earlobes. She released her hands and everything in her face dropped. There was no hate or disgust for the face she saw looking back at her. Maybe God really did have a plan for her. It might not be the one she wanted, but it would be the plan she needed.

She looked down from the mirror and returned her gaze to her hands. They were miraculous.

These two appendages were capable of so much more than she ever gave them credit for. They could comfort someone with a hug or with a simple touch. They could build a home for a family or tear down walls. They could hold a newborn baby or comfort a life near its end. Her two hands had the literal power to save a life or take one away. These hands were more than ready to face her eating disorder. If they had the ability to write her suicide letter, they had the ability to give her demon a name, a face, a persona to confront and conquer. These hands were ready to write the letter to her eating disorder.

She ran over towards her nightstand, opened the drawer, and grabbed a pen and paper. Sitting on the edge of her bed, Amelia began to write.

Dear Lauren,

For the last two years of my life, I've been your puppet, performing in your screwed up theatrical play. I've allowed you to dictate my thoughts, desires, wants, and actions. I used to hate you, yet I gave you more love and attention than you ever deserved.

I'd see you as this beautiful thing, one that had control and a thigh gap I envied, a screwed-up version of my reality where I believed this is what it meant to be beautiful, to be strong, and this was the only way I could ever be loved.

But now I see I was never empathizing with you; I was commiserating alongside you. I wasn't compassionate; I was codependent. Your familiarity and consistency provided me a comfort, dragging me down to your level. Now it's time for me to get uncomfortable and lean into it— to learn from the discomfort, not push away from it.

I have to learn the lesson behind your pain.

It was necessary for me to meet you. Your fragile arms that were barely able to pick yourself up when you fell to the ground time and time again. Your long brown hair tangled in a way that shows a lack of care. Your fingers that have grabbed ahold of the skin along your waist so hard it bled as a form of punishment for existing. You were necessary, because if I didn't experience a life with you, I wouldn't be where I am today.

Every little piece of the bigger puzzle matters. You are a part of my story, and that story has brought me to the exact point I'm at today. If I didn't know you, I wouldn't have been perfectly positioned in this universe to have adopted Luna. I wouldn't have ended up in Denver to start finding myself.

You will always be a part of my story, Lauren. But you are no longer the lead character. I am. You play a supporting role, teaching me what I'm made of, where I need to go, and that all of the struggles, pain, and hurt you have exposed me to has been worth it.

Today, I am thriving and not even you can take that away from me.

I love you, and I'm sorry you've been bottled up for so long. But I am no longer commiserating with you. I empathize with you and your brokenness. I'm compassionate towards your lack of self-love and desire to put everyone else before yourself. I'm in awe of the struggles you've had to endure while still managing to see the light of day.

But I think it's time we start working with each other rather than against each other. Dominic was a chapter in our story. Corey and Emmett were paragraphs. All the words are important, but they are not the story. I control the narrative from this point forward. I am the story.

Thank you for showing me where there is work that still needs to be done. Thank you for dragging me down to the bottom so I could see the place I never want to end up again. Thank you for every lesson you've taught and will continue to teach me. But don't take my kindness for weakness, not anymore.

Know this. I am my own savior, not you, Emmett, Dominic, or anyone else. I am more than ordinary, I am extraordinary.

We have a long road ahead of us, but I know that it's a road worth taking. We have to trust our body. Our body never lies. We just need to hold on a little longer.

Sincerely,

Amelia

Resources

If you or someone you know is suffering from an eating disorder or other mental health conditions, here are just a few of the numerous additional resources available where you can find education, support, and professional care for you or your loved one. This list is not exhaustive and many other resources and organizations are available along with what is listed. Many of these are located in the United States, but provide valuable information, resources, tools, and support for those all over the world.[1]

7 Cups
7cups.com

ADAA (Anxiety and Depression Association of America)
adaa.org

AED (Academy for Eating Disorders)
aedweb.org

AFSP (American Foundation for Suicide Prevention)
afsp.org

---

[1] *Please note that the author and publishers have no responsibility for the persistence or accuracy of URLs for external or third-party Internet Websites referred to in this publication and does not guarantee that any content on such Websites is, or will remain, accurate or appropriate.*

ANAD (National Association of Anorexia Nervosa and Associated Disorders)
anad.org

Depression and Bipolar Support Alliance
dbsalliance.org

EDF (Eating Disorder Foundation)
eatingdisorderfoundation.org

F.E.A.S.T. (Families Empowered and Supporting Treatment of Eating Disorders)
feast-ed.org

iaedp™ (International Association of Eating Disorder Professionals)
iaedp.com

It Gets Better Project
itgetsbetter.org

MHA (Mental Health America)
mhanational.org

NAMI (National Alliance on Mental Health)
nami.org

NEDA (National Eating Disorder Association)
nationaleatingdisorders.org

NIMH (National Institute of Mental Health)
nimh.nih.gov

Project HEAL
theprojectheal.org

Substance Abuse and Mental Health Services Administration
samhsa.gov

Suicide Prevention Lifeline
suicidepreventionlifeline.org

Trans Lifeline
translifeline.org

The Trevor Project
thetrevorproject.org

Acknowledgements

I look back at the person who started writing this book in the summer of 2020, during the midst of a global pandemic and in the beginning stages of my recovery. I guarantee she wouldn't believe me if I told her I'd have an entire village to thank for the creation of this book. If I were to acknowledge every person who has made an impact, I'd never stop writing.

To my family who made me, formed me, and challenged me to become the independent and courageous woman I am today.

Anna Dow, you are a queen. A true presence of light and love, I am blessed to have been paired with on this Earth.

Michael Dow, Daddy-O, you give me the space to breathe, the courage to be free, and the reassurance behind my doubt.

Jonathan, Alicia, and Kelly, our blood flows deeper than our hearts.

Haven, Paz, Gisele, Lily, Moses, Bijou, Mikayla, River, and Lucca, you kiddos are my heart, through and through.

Tim Porosky, I was drowning in the moment, and you kept me sober. Thank you for always answering the phone.

Chris Feld, there would be no book, no thought-dump, no possibility of saving myself without you. You are the reason I found what it took to thrive. I only hope that this book shows you how much you truly mean to me, and how much I undeniably miss you. Happy 11th birthday. You didn't did it; you done it.

Chelsea Wilde, Bryanna Hinkle, Joanna Vossahlik, Elli Mercer, Sven Hevia you were there from far beyond the beginning of this book, all the way through to the end. You were the first eyes on the very first chapter of this creation. Your brutal honesty has shaped me. Your never ending love has changed me. You are my chosen family. And I would choose the five of you every single time.

Timmy Miller, for listening to me talk about this book nonstop for a solid year, for holding me when I cried about how hard it was, and celebrating every small victory. Thank you for making the hard decisions. Thank you for it all. And to your family, for being on my team without even knowing me.

Taylor Fraser and Nicole Sylvester, the two of you took time out of your lives to not only read my book, but finish it with absolute love for a person you barely knew. You both read it in its rawest form, and still, you two women gave me the confidence I needed to put this book into the hands of others.

A special thank you to an amazing group of individuals who helped turn this book into something tangible for others to experience. Thank you to my outstanding editor, Claire Evans, to my kick-ass accountability partner for keeping me on track, Rhiannon Roberts, to Sterling Fraser for the countless hours you've spent teaching me and having my back, to Abigail Wilde for being the first to hear the words out loud, to Drew Rivera, PA-C for finding such value in this book reflected by your nomination of *In Body I Trust* for the Mental Health America 2021 Media Award, and to Jason Brueckner for sharing your knowledge, being my sounding board, and doing it all with nothing but undeniable compassion, space, and embrace.

To the advanced review readers, podcast hosts, bloggers, and incredibly beautiful human beings who have helped me continue my mission of normalizing mental health and reinforcing self-love, you are a part of this adventure and I couldn't be more grateful for each and every one of you.

Without the help of my therapist (who I'll leave anonymous for the sake of everyone's privacy) and my family at the Eating Disorder Foundation, I would've never been able to believe in a future for myself. What you all have done, and continue to do for so many people, is beyond words.

Thank you to every single person who preordered *In Body I Trust* to help benefit Project HEAL. Your contribution went to an incredible organization that is helping to break down systemic, healthcare, and financial barriers to eating disorder treatments, provide life-saving support to whom the system fails, and continue quantitative research for underrepresented populations. To learn more about what your contribution to Project HEAL is doing, visit theprojectheal.org.

I'd like to acknowledge the people who were there from the beginning of this journey. From the very real experiences I encountered that inspired this book to the moment I shared my story of recovery, hundreds of you have supported and encouraged me to keep going. To keep living. And to those of you who shared your personal stories with me, I'm honored that you trusted me to lean on. Your truths have been fuel to my fire towards this accomplishment.

Thank you to everyone throughout post-publication. One year ago, I didn't think I'd have as many individuals to thank. A year from now, I can only imagine how big my village will have become.

And last, but certainly not least, thank you, reader and new friend, for taking a chance on me. Thank you for picking up this creation of pain, love, and growth that we can now officially call a book. Surreal is as close to a name for this feeling as I can get. Thank you will never be enough for making my dreams a reality.

Lauren Dow is an author and founder of the independent publishing house, New Luna Press. She graduated from the University of South Florida in 2012 where she earned her bachelors in Public Relations. Her career has taken her to multiple countries throughout Europe and the Americas. In 2018 after being diagnosed with an eating disorder, she worked her way through recovery and has since dedicated her work to reinforcing self-love and providing support for individuals and families affected by mental health. Lauren is a dog mom to her four-legged child, Luna. Together they live on a cozy island in Tampa Bay.

Other works by Lauren Dow include *Your Wild Journal: 30 Days of Journal Prompts: Change Your Perspective & Discover Your Creativity.*

LaurenDow.com
Instagram: @laurendowwrites
Twitter: @laurendowwrites
Facebook.com/laurendowwrites